DEATH'S JEST-BOOK; OR, THE FOOL'S TRAGEDY

Published @ 2017 Trieste Publishing Pty Ltd

ISBN 9780649026609

Death's Jest-Book; Or, The Fool's Tragedy by Thomas Lovell Beddoes

Edited by Trieste Publishing Pty Ltd.
Cover @ 2017

www.triestepublishing.com

THOMAS LOVELL BEDDOES

DEATH'S JEST-BOOK; OR, THE FOOL'S TRAGEDY

DEATH'S JEST-BOOK

OR

THE FOOL'S TRAGEDY

ALDI

DISCIP.

ANGLVS

LONDON

WILLIAM PICKERING

1850

——— δημαγωγεῖ
ἐν τοῖς ἄνω νεκροῖσι,   420
κάστὶν τὰ πρῶτα τῆς ἐκεῖ μοχθηρίας.

*   *   *   *

Χωρῶμεν ἐς πολυρρόδους
λειμῶνας ἀνθεμώδεις,   450
  τὸν ἡμέτερον τρόπον,
  τὸν καλλιχορώτατον,
  παίζοντες, ὃν ὄλβιαι
  Μοῖραι ξυνάγουσιν.
ΜΟΝΟΙΣ ΓΑΡ ἩΜΙΝ ἩΛΙΟΣ
ΚΑΙ ΦΕΓΓΟΣ ἹΛΑΡΟΝ ἘΣΤΙΝ
  ὍΣΟΙ ΜΕΜΥΗΜΕΘ'.
      Χορος Μυστων.

Aristoph. Ranæ. Ed. Dindorf Oxon. 1833.

PERSONS REPRESENTED.

MELVERIC; Duke of MUNSTERBERG.
ADALMAR; } His sons.
ATHULF;
WOLFRAM; a knight. } Brothers.
ISBRAND; the court-fool.
THORWALD; Governor in the Duke's absence.
MARIO; a Roman.
SIEGFRIED; a courtier.
ZIBA; an Egyptian slave.
HOMUNCULUS MANDRAKE; Zany to a mountebank.

SIBYLLA.
AMALA; Thorwald's daughter.
IOAN.

*Knights, Ladies, Arabs, Priests, Sailors, Guards,
and other attendants.*
The Dance of Death.

SCENE; in the first act at Ancona, and afterwards in
Egypt: in the latter acts at the town of Grüssau,
residence of the Duke of Munsterberg, in Silesia.

TIME; the end of the thirteenth century.

DEATH'S JEST-BOOK;

OR THE FOOL'S TRAGEDY.

ACT I.

SCENE I. *Port of Ancona.*

Enter MANDRAKE *and* JOAN.

Mandr.

AM I a man of gingerbread that you should mould me to your liking? To have my way, in spite of your tongue and reason's teeth, tastes better than Hungary wine; and my heart beats in a honey-pot now I reject you and all sober sense: so tell my master, the doctor, he must seek another zany for his booth, a new wise merry Andrew. My jests are cracked, my coxcomb fallen, my bauble confiscated, my cap decapitated. Toll the bell; for oh! for oh! Jack Pudding is no more!

Joan. Wilt thou away from *me* then, sweet Mandrake? Wilt thou not marry me?

Mandr. Child, my studies must first be ended.
Thou knowest I hunger after wisdom, as the red sea
after ghosts : therefore will I travel awhile.

Joan. Whither, dainty Homunculus ?

Mandr. Whither should a student in the black arts,
a journeyman magician, a Rosicrucian ? Where is our
country ? You heard the herald this morning thrice
invite all christian folk to follow the brave knight, Sir
Wolfram, to the shores of Egypt, and there help to
free from bondage his noble fellow in arms, Duke
Melveric, whom, on a pilgrimage to the Holy Sepulchre, wild pagans captured. There, Joan, in that
Sphynx land found Raimund Lully those splinters of
the philosopher's stone with which he made English
Edward's gold. There dwell hoary magicians, who
have given up their trade and live sociably as croco-
diles on the banks of the Nile. There can one chat
with mummies in a pyramid, and breakfast on basilisk's
eggs. Thither then, Homunculus Mandrake, son of
the great Paracelsus; languish no more in the ignorance of these climes, but aboard with alembic and
crucible, and weigh anchor for Egypt.

Enter ISBRAND.

Isbr. Good morrow, brother Vanity! How ? soul
of a pickle-herring, body of a spagirical toss-pot, dou-
blet of motley, and mantle of pilgrim, how art thou
transmuted ! Wilt thou desert our brotherhood, fool

sublimate? Shall the motley chapter no longer boast
thee? Wilt thou forswear the order of the bell, and
break thy vows to Momus? Have mercy on Wisdom
and relent.

Mandr. Respect the grave and sober, I pray thee.
To-morrow I know thee not. In truth, I mark that
our noble faculty is in its last leaf. The dry rot of
prudence hath eaten the ship of fools to dust; she is
no more sea worthy. The world will see its ears in a
glass no longer; So we are laid aside and shall soon
be forgotten; for why should the feast of asses come
but once a year, when all the days are foaled of one
mother? O world, world! The gods and fairies left
thee, for thou wert too wise; and now, thou Socratic
star, thy demon, the great Pan, Folly, is parting from
thee. The oracles still talked in their sleep, shall our
grand-children say, till Master Merriman's kingdom
was broken up: now is every man his own fool, and
the world's sign is taken down.

(*He sings.*)
Folly hath now turned out of door
Mankind and Fate, who were before
    Jove's harlequin and clown:
For goosegrass-harvest now is o'er;
The world's no stage, no tavern more,
    Its sign, the Fool's ta'en down.

Isbr. Farewell, thou great-eared mind: I mark, by

thy talk, that thou commencest philosopher, and then
thou art only a fellow-servant out of livery.   But lo !
here come the uninitiated—.

(*Enter* THORWALD, AMALA, WOLFRAM, Knights
and Ladies.)

 Thorw. The turning tide ; the sea's wide leafless
   wind,
Wherein no birds inhabit and few traffic,
Making his cave within your sunny sails ;
The eager waves, whose golden, silent kisses
Seal an alliance with your bubbling oars ;
And our still-working wishes, that impress
Their meaning on the conscience of the world,
And prompt the unready Future,—all invite you
Unto your voyage.   Prosperous be the issue,
As is the promise, and the purpose good !
Are all the rest aboard ?
 Wolfr.   All.   'Tis a band
Of knights, whose bosoms pant with one desire,
And live but in the hope to free their prince :
All hearts beat merrily, all arms are ready.
 Mandr. All, sir Knight ; even the very pigs and
capons, and poor dear great Mandrake must be shipped
too.
 Wolfr. Who is this saucy fellow, that prates be-
  tween ?
 Isbr. One of the many you have made.   Yesterday

ıs a fellow of my colour and served a quacksalver,
ıow he lusts after the mummy country, whither
ıre bound. 'Tis a servant of the rosy cross, a cor-
ndent of the stars; the dead are his boon com-
ns, and the secrets of the moon his knowledge.
had I been cook to a chameleon, I could not
ıen the air to his praise enough. Suffice it, of
ısdom Solomon knew less than a bee of fossil
rs, or the ambrosian demigods of table beer. We
send him as our ambassador to Africa; take him
you, or be yourself our consul.

'olfr. Aboard then in all speed; and sink us not
thy understanding.

'andr. I thank thee, Knight. Twice shalt thou
'or this, if I bottle eternity.   [*Exit, with* JOAN.

horw. These letters yet, full of most weighty
          secrets:
ırein, of what I dare but whisper to thee,
ǝ the dissemblers listen to our speech;
is two sons, whose love and dread ambition,
sing like deadly swords, teach us affright;
  of the uncertain people, who incline
y more to the present influence,
ǝetting all that their sense apprehends not;
ve at large discoursed unto the duke:
. may you find his spirit strong to bear
  bending load of such untoward tidings,
ınust press hard upon him.

Amala.   And forget not
Our duke, with gentle greetings, to remind
Of those who have no sword to raise for him,
But whose unarmed love is not less true,
Than theirs who seek him helmed.   Farewell, sir
       knight;
They say you serve a lady in those lands,
So we dare offer you no token else
But our good wishes.
    Wolfr.   Thanks, and farewell to all;
And so I take my leave.
    Amala.   We to our homes;
You to the homeless waves; unequal parting.
    Wolfr. The earth may open, and the sea o'erwhelm;
Many the ways, the little home is one;
Thither the courser leads, thither the helm,
And at one gate we meet when all is done.
          [*Exeunt all but* WOLFRAM *and* ISBRAND.
    Isbr. Stay: you have not my blessing yet.   With
what jest shall I curse you in earnest?   Know you this
garb, and him who wears it, and wherefore it is worn?
A father slain and plundered; a sister's love first worn
in the bosom, then trampled in the dust : our fraternal
bond, shall it so end that thou savest him whom we
should help to damn?   O do it, and I shall learn to
laugh the dead out of their coffins !
    Wolfr. Hence with your dark demands : let's shape
       our lives
After the merciful lesson of the sun,

That gilds our purpose. See the dallying waves
Caress invitingly into their bosom
. My fleet ship's keel, that at her anchor bounds
As doth the greyhound at her leader's hand,
Following her eye beams after the light roe.

Isbr. Away then, away! Thus perish our good
Revenge! Unfurl your sails: let all the honest finny
folk of ocean, and those fair witty spinsters, the mermaids, follow your luckless boats with mockery : sea
serpents and sea-dogs and venomous krakens have
mercy on your mercy, and drag you down to the salt
water element of pity! What, O! what spirit of our
ancestral enemies would dare to whisper through our
father's bones the tale of thy apostacy? Deliver *him*
from the Saracens' irons, or the coil of the desert snake,
who robbed our sire's grey hairs of a kingdom, his
heart of its best loved daughter, and trod him down a
despairing beggar to the crowned corpses of our pro-
genitors? Save *him*, who slew our hopes; who co-
zened us of our share of this sepulchral planet, whereon
our statues should have stood sceptred? Revenge,
Revenge lend me your torch, that I may by its bloody
fire see the furrows of this man's countenance, which
once were iron, like the bars of Hell gate, and devilish
thoughts peeped through them; but now are as a cage
of very pitiful apes.

Wolfr. Should we repent this change? I know
    not why.
We came disguised into the court, stiff limbed

With desperate intent, and doubly souled
With murder's devil and our own still ghosts.
But must I not relent, finding the heart,
For which my dagger hungered, so inclined
In brotherly affection unto me?
O bless the womanish weakness of my soul,
Which came to slay, and leads me now to save!

Isbr. Hate! Hate! Revenge and blood! These
are the first words my boys shall learn. What accursed poison has that Duke, that snake, with his
tongue, his fang, dropped into thine ear? Thou art no
brother of mine more: his soul was of that tune which
shall awaken the dead: for thine! if I could make a
trumpet of the devil's antlers, and blow thee through
it, my lady's poodle would be scarce moved to a horn-
pipe. O fie on't! Thou my brother? Say when hast
thou undergone transfusion, and whose hostile blood
now turns thy life's wheels? Who has poured Lethe
into thy veins, and washed thy father out of heart and
brains? Ha! be pale, and smile, and be prodigal of
thy body's movements, for thou hast no soul more.
That thy sire placed in thee; and, with the determi-
nation to avenge him, thou hast driven it out of doors.
But 'tis well so: why lament? Now I have all the
hatred and revenge of the world to myself to abhor
and murder him with.

Wolfr. Thou speak'st unjustly, what thou rashly
        think'st;

But time must soften and convince : now leave me,
If thou hast nothing but reproach for pastime.

Isbr. Be angry then, and we will curse each other.
But if thou goest now to deliver this man, come not
again for fear of me and our father's spirit: for when
he visits me in the night, screaming revenge, my heart
forgets that my head wears a fool's cap, and dreams of
daggers : come not again then !

Wolfr. O think not, brother, that our father's spirit
Breathes earthy passion more : he is with me
And guides me to the danger of his foe,
Bringing from heaven, his home, pity and pardon.
But, should his blood need bloody expiation,
Then let *me* perish.   Blind these eyes, my sire,
Palsy my vigorous arm, snow age upon me,
Strike me with lightning down into the deep,
Open me any grave that earth can spare,
Leave me the truth of love, and death is lovely.
                                            [*Exit.*

Isbr. O lion-heartedness right asinine !
Such lily-livered meek humanity
Saves not thy duke, good brother ; it but shines
Sickly upon his doom, as moonbeams breaking
Upon a murderer's grave-digging spade.
Or fate's a fool, or I will be his fate.
What ho !   Sir Knight !   One word—Now for a face
As innocent and lamblike as the wool
That brings a plague.

(Re-enter WOLFRAM.)

Wolfr. What will you more with me?

Isbr. Go, if you must and will; but take with you
At least this letter of the governor's,
Which, in your haste, you dropped. I must be honest,
For so my hate was ever. Go.

Wolfr.   And prosper!
                                            [*Exit.*

Isbr. Now then he plunges right into the waters!
O Lie, O Lie, O lovely lady Lie,
They told me that thou art the devil's daughter.
Then thou art greater than thy father, Lie;
For while he mopes in Hell, thou queen'st it bravely,
Ruling the earth under the name of Truth,
While she is at the bottom of the well,
Where Joseph left her.

Song from the ship.

To sea, to sea! The calm is o'er;
  The wanton water leaps in sport,
And rattles down the pebbly shore;
  The dolphin wheels, the sea-cows snort,
And unseen Mermaids' pearly song
Comes bubbling up, the weeds among.
  Fling broad the sail, dip deep the oar:
  To sea, to sea! the calm is o'er.

To sea, to sea! our wide-winged bark
  Shall billowy cleave its sunny way,

And with its shadow, fleet and dark,
   Break the caved Tritons' azure day,
Like mighty eagle soaring light
O'er antelopes on Alpine height.
   The anchor heaves, the ship swings free,
   The sails swell full. To sea, to sea!

Isbr. The idiot merriment of thoughtless men!
How the fish laugh at them, that swim and toy
About the ruined ship, wrecked deep below,
Whose pilot's skeleton, all full of sea weeds,
Leans on his anchor, grinning like their Hope.
But I will turn my bosom now to thee,
Brutus, thou saint of the avenger's order;
Refresh me with thy spirit, or pour in
Thy whole great ghost. Isbrand, thou tragic fool,
Cheer up. Art thou alone? Why so should be
Creators and destroyers. I'll go brood,
And strain my burning and distracted soul
Against the naked spirit of the world,
Till some portent's begotten.   [*Exit.*

SCENE II.

*The African Coast: a woody solitude near the sea.
In the back ground ruins overshadowed by the
characteristic vegetation of the oriental regions.*

The DUKE *and* SIBYLLA ; *the latter sleeping in
a tent.*

Duke. Soft sleep enwrap thee: with his balm bedew
Thy young fair limbs, Sibylla: thou didst need
The downy folding of his arms about thee.
And wake not yet, for still the starless night
Of our misfortune holds its ghostly noon.
No serpent shall creep o'er the sand to sting thee,
No springing tiger, no uncouth sea-monster,
(For such are now the partners of thy chamber,)
Disturb thy rest: only the birds shall dare
To shake the sparkling blossoms that hang o'er thee,
And fan thee with their wings. As I watch for thee,
So may the power, that has so far preserved us,
Now in the uttermost, now that I feel
The cold drops on my forehead, and scarce know
Whether Fear shed them there, or the near breath
Of our pursuing foes has settled on it,
Stretch its shield o'er us.

Enter ZIBA.

What bring'st, Ziba? Hope?
Else be as dumb as that thou bring'st, Despair.
Ziba. Fruits: as I sat among the boughs, and robbed
The sparrows and their brothers of their bread,
A horde of casqued Saracens rode by,
Each swearing that thy sword should rest ere night
Within his sheath, his weapon in thy breast.
Duke. Speak lower, Ziba, lest the lady wake.
Perhaps she sleeps not, but with half-shut eyes
Will hear her fate. The slaves shall need to wash
My sword of Moslem blood before they sheath it.
Which path took they?
Ziba. Sleeping, or feigning sleep,
Well done of her: 'tis trying on a garb
Which she must wear, sooner or later, long:
'Tis but a warmer lighter death. The ruffians,
Of whom I spoke, turned towards the cedar forest,
And, as they went in, there rushed forth a lion
And tore their captain down. Long live the lion!
We'll drink his tawny health: he gave us wine.
For, while the Moors in their black fear were flying,
I crept up to the fallen wretch, and borrowed
His flask of rubious liquor. May the prophet
Forgive him, as I do, for carrying it!
This for to-day: to-morrow hath gods too,
Who'll ripen us fresh berries, and uncage
Another lion on another foe.

Duke. Brave Arab, thanks.   But saw'st thou from
    the heights
No christian galley steering for this coast ?

Ziba. I looked abroad upon the wide old world,
And in the sky and sea, through the same clouds,
The same stars saw I glistening, and nought else.
And as my soul sighed unto the world's soul,
Far in the north a wind blackened the waters,
And, after that creating breath was still,
A dark speck sat on the sky's edge : as watching
Upon the heaven-girt border of my mind
The first faint thought of a great deed arise,
With force and fascination I drew on
The wished sight, and my hope seemed to stamp
Its shape upon it.   Not yet is it clear
What, or from whom, the vessel.

Duke.   Liberty !
Thou breakest through our dungeon's wall of waves,
As morning bursts the towery spell of night.
Horse of the desert, thou, coy arrowy creature,
Startest like sunrise up, and, from thy mane
Shaking abroad the dews of slumber, boundest
With sparkling hoof along the scattered sands,
The livelong day in liberty and light.
But see, the lady stirs.   Once more look out,
And thy next news be safety.   [*Exit* ZIBA.
                              Hast thou gathered
Rest and refreshment from thy desert couch,
My fair Sibylla ?

Sibyl.   Deeply have I slept.
As one who hath gone down unto the springs
Of his existence and there bathed, I come
Regenerate up into the world again.
Kindest protector, 'tis to thee I owe
This boon, a greater than my parents gave.
Me, who had never seen this earth, this heaven,
The sun, the stars, the flowers, but shut from nature
Within my dungeon birthplace lived in darkness,
Me hast thou freed from the oppressor's chain,
And godlike given me this heaven, this earth,
The flowers, the stars, the sun.   Methinks it were
Ingratitude to thank thee for a gift
So measurelessly great.
    Duke.   As yet, sweet lady,
I have deserved but little thanks of thine.
We've not yet broken prison.   This wall of waves
Still towers between us and the world of men:
That too I hope to climb.   Our true Egyptian
Hath brought me news of an approaching ship.
When that hath borne thee to our German shore,
And thou amongst the living tastest life,
And gallants shall have shed around thy presence
A glory of the starry looks of love,
For thee to move in, thank me then.
    Sibyl.   I wish not
To leave this shady quiet bower of life.
Why should we seek cruel mankind again?

Nature is kinder far: and every thing
That lives around us, with its pious silence,
Gives me delight: the insects, and the birds
· That come unto our table, seeking food,
The flowers, upon whose petals Night lays down
Her dewy necklace, are my dearest playmates.
O let us never leave them.
    Duke.   That would be
To rob thy fate of thee. In other countries
Another godliker mankind doth dwell,
Whose works each day adorn and deify
The world their fathers left them. Thither shalt tho
For among them must be the one thou'rt born for.
Durst thou be such a traitress to thy beauty
As to live here unloving and unloved?
    Sibyl. Love I not thee? O, if I feel beside thee
Content and an unruffled calm, in which
My soul doth gather round thee, to reflect
Thy heavenly goodness: if I feel my heart
So full of comfort near thee, that no room
For any other wish, no doubt, remains;
Love I not thee?
    Duke.   Dear maiden, thou art young.
Thou must see many, and compare their merits
Ere thou canst choose. Esteem and quiet friendshi
Oft bear Love's semblance for awhile.
    Sibyl.   I know it;
Thou shalt hear how. A year and more is past

Since a brave Saxon knight did share our prison;
A noble generous man, in whose discourse
I found much pleasure: yet, when he was near me,
There ever was a pain which I could taste
Even in the thick and sweetest of my comfort:
Strange dread of meeting, greater dread of parting:
My heart was never still: and many times,
When he had fetched me flowers, I trembled so
That oft they fell as I was taking them
Out of his hand.   When I would speak to him
I heard not, and I knew not what I said.
I saw his image clearer in his absence
Than near him, for my eyes were strangely troubled;
And never had I dared to talk thus to him.
Yet this I thought was Love.   O self deceived!
For now I can speak all I think to thee
With confidence and ease.   What else can that be
Except true love?
     Duke.   The like I bear to thee,
O more than all that thou hast promised me:
For if another being stepped between us,
And were he my best friend, I must forget
All vows, and cut his heart away from mine.
     Sibyl. Think not on that: it is impossible.
     Duke. Yet, my Sibylla, oft first love must perish;
Like the poor snow-drop, boyish love of Spring,
Born pale to die, and strew the path of triumph

c

Before the imperial glowing of the rose,
Whose passion conquers all.

Enter ZIBA.

Ziba. O my dear lord, we're saved!
Duke.   How? Speak quickly.
Though every word hath now no meaning in't,
Since thou hast said ' she's saved.'
  Ziba. The ship is in the bay, a christian knight
Steps from his boat upon the shore.
  Duke.   Blest hour!
And yet how palely, with what faded lips
Do we salute this unhoped change of fortune!
Thou art so silent, lady; and I utter
Shadows of words, like to an ancient ghost,
Arisen out of hoary centuries
Where none can speak his language. I had thought
That I should laugh, and shout, and leap on high:
But see this breath of joy hath damped my soul,
Melted the icy mail, with which despair
Had clad my heart and sealed the springs of weakness:
And O! how feeble, faint, and sad I go
To welcome what I prayed for. Thou art silent;
How art thou then, my love?
  Sibyl.   Now Hope and Fear
Stand by me, masked in one another's shapes;
I know not which is which, and, if I did,
I doubt which I should choose.

Enter a Knight.

Knight. Hither, Sir Knight—

Duke.   What knight?

Knight.   What knight, but Wolfram?

Duke. Wolfram, *my* knight !

Sibyl.   My day, my Wolfram !

Duke.   Know'st him ?

Sibyl. His foot is on my heart ; he comes, he comes.

Enter WOLFRAM, *knights and attendants.*

Wolfr. Are these thy comrades ?

Then, Arab, thy life's work and mine is done.

My duke, my brother knight !

Duke.   O friend ! So call me !

Wolfram, thou comest to us like a god,

Giving life where thou touchest with thy hand.

Wolfr. Were it mine own, I'd break it here in twain,

And give you each a half.

Duke.   I will not thank thee,

I will not welcome thee, embrace and bless thee ;

Nor will I weep in silence.   Gratitude,

Friendship, and Joy are beggar'd, and turned forth

Out of my heart for shallow hypocrites :

They understand me not; and my soul, dazzled,

Stares on the unknown feelings that now crowd it,

Knows none of them, remembers none, counts none,

More than a new-born child in its first hour.

One word, and then we'll speak of this no more :

At parting each of us did tear a leaf
Out of a magic book, and, robbing life
Of the red juice with which she feeds our limbs,
We wrote a mutual bond. Dost thou remember?

Wolfr. And if a promise reaches o'er the grave
My ghost shall not forget it. There I swore
That, if I died before thee, I would come
With the first weeds that shoot out of my grave,
And bring thee tidings of our real home.

Duke. That bond hast thou now cancelled thus; or
    rather
Unto me lying in my sepulchre
Comest thou, and say'st, " Arise and live again."

Wolfr. And with thee dost thou bring some angel
    back.
Look on me, lady.

Sibyl (aside).   Pray heaven, it be not
The angel of the death of one of you,
To make the grave and the flowers' roots amends.
Now turn I to thee, knight. O dared I hope,
Thou hast forgotten me !

Wolfr.   Then dead indeed
Were I, and my soul disinherited
Of immortality, which love of thee
Gave me the proof of first. Forgotten thee !
Ay; if thou be not she, with whom I shared
Few months ago that dungeon, which thy presence
Lit with delight unknown to liberty;

If thou be not Sibylla, she whose semblance
Here keepeth watch upon my breast.   Behold it:
Morning and night my heart doth beat against it.
Thou gavest it me one day, when I admired,
Above all crystal gems, a dewdrop globe
Which, in the joyous dimple of a flower,
Imaged thee tremulously.   Since that time
Many a secret tear hath mirrored thee,
And many a thought, over this pictured beauty.
Speak to me then: or art thou, as this toy,
Only the likeness of the maid I loved?
But there's no seeming such a one.   O come!
This talking is a pitiful invention:
We'll leave it to the wretched.   All my science,
My memory, I'd give for this one joy,
And keep it ever secret.
  Sibyl.   Wolfram, thou movest me:
With soul-compelling looks thou draw'st me to thee:
O! at thy call I must surrender me,
My lord, my love, my life.
  Duke.   Thy life! O lives, that dwell
In these three bosoms, keep your footings fast,
For there's a blasting thought stirring among you.
They love each other.   Silence!   Let them love;
And let him be her love.   She is a flower,
Growing upon a grave.   Now, gentle lady,
Retire, beseech you, to the tent and rest.
My friend and I have need to use those words

Which are bequeathed unto the miserable.
Come hither; you have made me master of them :
Who dare be wretched in the world beside me ?
Think now what you have done; and tremble at it.
But I forgive thee, love.   Go in and rest thee.

    Sibyl.   And he ?

    Duke.   Is he not mine ?

    Wolfr.   Go in, sweet, fearlessly.

I come to thee, before thou'st time to feel
That I am absent.

             [Exit SIBYLLA, *followed by the rest.*

    Duke.   Wolfram, we have been friends.

    Wolfr.   And will be ever.

I know no other way to live.

    Duke.   'Tis pity.

I would you had been one day more at sea.

    Wolfr.   Why so ?

    Duke.   You're troublesome to-day.   Have you not
    marked it ?

    Wolfr.   Alas ! that you should say so.

    Duke.   That's all needless.

Those times are past, forgotten.   Hear me, knight :
That lady's love is mine.   Now you know that,
Do what you dare.

    Wolfr. ·   The lady ! my Sibylla !

I would I did not love thee for those words,
That I might answer well.

    Duke.   Unless thou yield'st her—

For thou hast even subdued her to thy arms,
Against her will and reason, wickedly
Torturing her soul with spells and adjurations,—
Unless thou giv'st her the free will again
To take her natural course of being on,
Which flowed towards me with gentle love:—O Wol-
    fram,
Thou know'st not how she filled my soul so doing,
Even as the streams an ocean:—Give her me,
And we are friends again.   But I forget:
Thou lovest her too; a stern, resolved rival;
And passionate, I know.   Nay then, speak out:
'Twere better that we argued warmly here,
Till the blood has its way.

    Wolfr.   Unworthy friend!
My lord—

    Duke.   Forget that I am so, and many things
Which we were to each other, and speak out.
I would we had much wine; 'twould bring us sooner
To the right point.

    Wolfr.   Can it be so?   O Melveric!
I thought thou wert the very one of all
Who shouldst have heard my secret with delight.
I thought thou wert my friend.

    Duke.   Such things as these,
Friendship, esteem, faith, hope, and sympathy,
We need no more: away with them for ever!
Wilt follow them out of the world?   Thou see'st

All human things die and decay around us.
'Tis the last day for us; and we stand bare
To let our cause be tried. See'st thou not why?
We love one creature: which of us shall tear her
Out of his soul? I have in all the world
Little to comfort me, few that do name me
With titles of affection, and but one
Who came into my soul at its night-time,
As it hung glistening with starry thoughts
Alone over its still eternity,
And gave it godhead. Thou art younger far,
More fit to be beloved; when thou appearest
All hearts incline to thee, all prouder spirits
Are troubled unto tears and yearn to love thee.
O, if thou knew'st thy heart-compelling power,
Thou wouldst not envy me the only creature
That holds me dear. If I were such as thou,
I would not be forgetful of our friendship,
But yield to the abandoned his one joy.

Wolfr. Thou prob'st me to the quick: before to-day,
Methought thou could'st from me nothing demand
And I refuse it.

Duke.   Wolfram, I do beseech thee;
The love of her's my heaven; thrust me not from her;
I have no hope elsewhere: thrust me not from her;
Or thou dost hurl me into hell's embrace,
Making me the devil's slave to thy perdition.

Wolfr. O, would to heaven,

That I had found thee struggling in a battle,
Alone against the swords of many foes!
Then had I rescued thee, and died content,
Ignorant of the treasure I had saved thee.
But now my fate hath made a wisher of me:
O woe that so it is! O woe to wish
That she had never been, who is the cause!

   Duke. He is the cause! O fall the curse on him,
And may he be no more, who dares the gods
With such a wish! Speak thou no more of love,
No more of friendship here: the world is open:
I wish you life and merriment enough
From wealth and wine, and all the dingy glory
Fame doth reward those with, whose love-spurned hearts
Hunger for goblin immortality.
Live long, grow old, and honour crown thy hairs,
When they are pale and frosty as thy heart.
Away. I have no better blessing for thee.
Wilt thou not leave me?

   Wolfr.   Should I leave thee thus?

   Duke. Why not? or must I hate thee perfectly?
And tell thee so? Away now I beseech you!
Have I not cut all ties betwixt us off?
Why, wert thou my own soul, I'd drive thee from me.
Go, put to sea again.

   Wolfr.   Farewell then, Duke.
Methinks thy better self indeed hath parted,
And that I follow.   [*Exit.*

Duke.   Thither? Thither? Traitor
To every virtue. Ha! What's this thought,
Shapeless and shadowy, that keeps wheeling round,
Like a dumb creature that sees coming danger,
And breaks its heart trying in vain to speak?
I know the moment: 'tis a dreadful one,
Which in the life of every one comes once;
When, for the frighted hesitating soul,
High heaven and luring sin with promises
Bid and contend: oft the faltering spirit,
O'ercome by the fair fascinating fiend,
Gives her eternal heritage of life
For one caress, for one triumphant crime.—
Pitiful villain! that dost long to sin,
And dar'st not. Shall I dream my soul is bathing
In his reviving blood, yet lose my right,
My only health, my sole delight on earth,
For fear of shadows on a chapel wall
In some pale painted Hell? No: by thy beauty,
I will possess thee, maiden. Doubt and care
Be trampled in the dust with the worm conscience!
Farewell then, Wolfram: now Amen is said
Unto thy time of being in this world:
Thou shalt die. Ha! the very word doth double
My strength of life: the resolution leaps
Into my heart divinely, as doth Mars
Upon the trembling footboard of his car,
Hurrying into battle wild and panting,

Even as my death-dispensing thought does now.
Ho! Ziba!

Enter ZIBA.

                    Hush!   How still, how full, how lightly
I move since this resolve, about the place,
Like to a murder-charged thunder cloud
Lurking about the starry streets of night,
Breathless and masked,
O'er a still city sleeping by the sea.
Ziba, come hither; thou'rt the night I'll hang
My muffled wrath in.   Come, I'll give thee work
Shall make thy life still darker, for one light on't
Must be put out.   O let me joy no more,
Till Fate hath kissed my wooing soul's desire
Off her death-honied lips, and so set seal
To my decree, in which he's sepulchred.
Come, Ziba, thou must be my counsellor.

                                        [*Exeunt.*

SCENE III.

A Tent on the sea-shore: sun-set.

WOLFRAM *and* SIBYLLA.

Wolfr. This is the oft-wished hour, when we to-
    . gether
May walk upon the sea-shore: let us seek

Some greensward overshadowed by the rocks.
Wilt thou come forth? Even now the sun is setting
In the triumphant splendour of the waves.
Hear you not how they leap?

    Sibyl.   Nay; we will watch
The sun go down upon a better day:
Look not on him this evening.

    Wolfr.   Then let's wander
Under the mountain's shade in the deep valley,
And mock the woody echoes with our songs.

    Sibyl. That wood is dark, and all the mountain caves
Dreadful, and black, and full of howling winds:
Thither we will not wander.

    Wolfr.   Shall we seek
The green and golden meadows, and there pluck
Flowers for thy couch, and shake the dew out of them?

    Sibyl. The snake that loves the twilight is come out,
Beautiful, still, and deadly; and the blossoms
Have shed their fairest petals in the storm
Last night; the meadow's full of fear and danger.

    Wolfr. Ah! you will to the rocky fount, and there
We'll see the fire-flies dancing in the breeze,
And the stars trembling in the trembling water,
And listen to the daring nightingale
Defying the old night with harmony.

    Sibyl. Nor that: but we will rather here remain,
And earnestly converse. What said the Duke?
Surely no good.

Wolfr.   A few unmeaning words,
I have almost forgotten.
Sibyl.   Tell me truly,
Else I may fear much worse.
Wolfr.   Well: it may be
That he was somewhat angry. 'Tis no matter;
He must soon cool and be content.

Enter ZIBA.

Ziba.   Hail, knight!
I bring to thee the draught of welcome. Taste it.
The Grecian sun ripened it in the grape,
Which Grecian maidens plucked and pressed: then
            came
The desert Arab to the palace gate,
And took it for his tribute. It is charmed;
And they who drink of such have magic dreams.
Wolfr. Thanks for thy care. I'll taste it presently:
Right honey for such bees as I.

Enter a Knight.

Knight.   Up, brave Wolfram!
Arouse thee, and come forth to help and save.
Wolfr. Here is my sword. Who needs it?
Sibyl.   Is't the Duke?
O my dark Fear!
Knight.   'Tis he. Hunting in the forest,
A band of robbers rushed on us.

Wolfr.   How many?

Knight. Some twelve to five of us; and in the fight,
Which now is at the hottest, my sword failed me.
Up, good knight, in all speed: I'll lead the way.

Wolfr. Sibylla, what deserves he at our hands?

Sibyl. Assist him; he preserved me.

Wolfr.   For what end?

Sibyl. Death's sickle points thy questions.   No
    delay:
But hence.

                Enter a second Knight.

Wolfr. Behold another from the field,—
Thy news?

2nd *Knight.* My fellow soldiers all
Bleed and grow faint: fresh robbers pour upon us,
And the Duke stands at bay unhelmed against them.

Wolfr. Brave comrade, keep the rogues before thee,
    dancing
At thy sword's point, but a few moments longer;
Then I am with thee.   Farewell thou, Sibylla;
He shall not perish thus.   Rise up, my men,
To horse with sword and spear, and follow flying.
I pledge thee, lady.   *(takes the goblet)*

  Ziba (dashing it to the ground). Flow wine, like
    Moorish gore.
Ha! it rings well and lies not.   'Tis right metal
For funeral bells.

Wolfr.   Slave, what hast thou done?

Ziba. Pour thou unto the subterranean gods
Libations of thy blood: I have shed wine.
Now, will ye not away?
 Wolfr.   Come hither, dark one:
Say, on thy life, why hast thou spilt that wine?
 Ziba. A superstitious fancy: but now hence.
'Twas costly liquor too.
 Wolfr.   Then finish it.
'Twas well that fortune did reserve for you
These last and thickest drops here at the bottom.
 Ziba. Drink them? forbid the prophet!
 Wolfr.   Slave, thou diest else.
 Ziba. Give me the beaker then.—O God, I dare
   not.
Death is too bitter so: alas! 'tis poison.
 Sibyl. Pernicious caitiff!
 Wolfr.   Patience, my Sibylla!
I knew it by thy lying eye. Thou'rt pardoned.
I may not tread upon the toothless serpent.
But for thy lord, the Saracen deal with him
As he thinks fit. Wolfram can aid no murderer.
 Sibyl. Mercy! O let me not cry out in vain:
Forgive him yet.
 Wolfr.   The crime I do forgive:
And Heaven, if he's forgiven there, preserve him!
O monstrous! in the moment when my heart
Looked back on him with the old love again,
Then was I marked for slaughter by his hand.

Forgive him? 'Tis enough: 'tis much. Lie still
Thou sworded hand, and thou be steely, heart.

Enter a third Knight *wounded.*

3rd *Knight.* Woe! woe! Duke Melveric is the
    Arabs' captive.
Sibyl. Then Heaven have mercy on him!
Wolfr.   So 'tis best:
He was o'erthrown and mastered by his passion,
As by a tiger. Death will burst the fetters.
3rd *Knight.* They bind him to a pillar in the de-
    sart,
And aim their poisoned arrows at his heart.
Wolfr. O Melveric, why didst thou so to me?
Sibylla, I despise this savage Duke,
But thus he shall not die. No man in bonds
Can be my enemy. He once was noble;
Once very noble. Let me set him free,
And we can then be knightly foes again.
Up, up, my men, once more and follow me.
I bring him to thee, love, or ne'er return.
    Sibyl. A thousand tearful thanks for this. O
        Wolfram!
                                [Exeunt severally.

Scene IV.

A forest: the moonlit sea glistens between the trees.

Enter Arabs *with the* Duke.

1st *Arab.* Against this column : there's an ancient beast
Here in the neighbourhood, which to-night will thank us
For the ready meal.

      [*they bind the Duke against a column.*
2nd *Arab.*   Christian, to thy houris
Boast that we took thy blood in recompense
Of our best comrades.

1st *Arab.*   Hast a saint or mistress?
Call on them, for next minute comes the arrow.

Duke. O Wolfram! now methinks thou lift'st the
      cup.
Strike quickly, Arab.

1st. *Arab.*   Brothers, aim at him.

Enter WOLFRAM *and knights.*

Wolfr. Down, murderers, down.
2nd *Arab.* Fly! there are hundreds on us.

      (*Fight—the Arabs are beaten out and pur-
      sued by the knights.*)

D

Wolfr. (*unbinding the Duke*) Thank heaven, not
   too late ! Now you are free.
There is your life again.
   Duke.   Hast thou drunk wine?
Answer me, knight, hast thou drunk wine this evening?
   Wolfr. Nor wine, nor poison.   The slave told me
   all.
O Melveric, if I deserve it from thee,
Now canst thou mix my draught.   But be't forgotten.
   Duke. And wilt thou not now kill me?
   Wolfr.   Let us strive
Henceforward with good deeds against each other,
And may you conquer there.   Hence, and for ever,
No one shall whisper of that deadly thought.
Now we will leave this coast.
   Duke.   Ay, we will step
Into a boat and steer away: but whither?
Think'st thou I'll live in the vile consciousness
That I have dealt so wickedly and basely,
And been of thee so like a god forgiven?
No: 'tis impossible . . Friend, by your leave—
       [*takes a sword from a fallen Arab.*
O what a coward villain must I be,
So to exist.
   Wolfr.   Be patient but awhile,
And all such thoughts will soften.
   Duke.   The grave be patient,
That's yawning at our feet for one of us.

I want no comfort. I am comfortable,
As any soul under the eaves of Heaven :
For one of us must perish in this instant.
Fool, would thy virtue shame and crush me down ;
And make a grateful blushing bondslave of me ?
O no ! I dare be wicked still : the murderer,
My thought has christened me, I must remain.
O curse thy meek, forgiving, idiot heart,
That thus must take its womanish revenge,
And with the loathliest poison, pardon, kill me :
Twice-sentenced, die !   [*Strikes at Wolfram.*
    Wolfr.   Madman, stand off.
    Duke. I pay my thanks in steel.
Thus be all pardoners pardoned.
                            [*Fight: Wolfram falls.*
    Wolfr. Murderer ! mine and my father's ! O my
        brother,
Too true thy parting words . . Repent thou never !
    Duke. So then we both are blasted : but thou diest,
Who daredst to love athwart my love, discover,
And then forgive, my treachery.   Now proclaim me.
Let my name burn through all dark history
Over the waves of time, as from a light-house,
Warning approach.   My worldly work is done.

            ZIBA *runs in.*

    Ziba. They come, they come ; if thy thought be not
        yet

Incarnate in a deed, it is too late.
Is it a deed?

Duke.   Look at me.

Ziba.   'Tis enough.

Duke. See'st? Know'st? Be silent and be gone.

                    [*Ziba retires: the knights re-enter*
                              with SIBYLLA.

Knight. O luckless victory! our leader wounded!

Sibyl. Bleeding to death! and he, whom he gave
    life to,
Even his own, unhurt and armed! Speak, Wolfram:
Let me not think thou'rt dying.

Wolfr.   But I am:
Slain villanously. Had I stayed, Sibylla—
But thou and life are lost; so I'll be silent.

Sibyl. O Melveric, why kneel'st not thou beside him?
Weep'st not with me? For thee he fell. O speak!
Who did this, Wolfram?

Wolfr.   'Tis well done, my Sibylla:
So burst the portals of sepulchral night
Before the immortal rising of the sun.

Sibyl. Who did this, Melveric?

Duke.   Let him die in quiet.
Hush! there's a thought upon his lips again.

Wolfr. A kiss, Sibylla! I ne'er yet have kissed
    thee,
And my new bride, death's lips are cold, they say.
Now it is darkening.

Sibyl.   O not yet, not yet !

Who did this, Wolfram?

Wolfr.   *Thou* know'st, Melveric :

At the last day reply thou to that question,

When such an angel asks it : I'll not answer

Or then or now.   [*Dies.*

    (*Sibylla throws herself on the body ; the Duke

    stands motionless ; the rest gather round in

    silence.   The scene closes.*)

A voice from the waters.

The swallow leaves her nest,

The soul my weary breast ;

But therefore let the rain

   On my grave

Fall pure ; for why complain ?

Since both will come again

   O'er the wave.

The wind dead leaves and snow

Doth hurry to and fro ;

And, once, a day shall break

   O'er the wave,

When a storm of ghosts shall shake

The dead, until they wake

   In the grave.

ACT II.

SCENE I.

The interior of a church at Ancona. The DUKE, *in the garb of a pilgrim,* SIBYLLA *and Knights, assembled round the corpse of Wolfram, which is lying on a bier.*

Dirge.

IF thou wilt ease thine heart
Of love and all its smart,
    Then sleep, dear, sleep;
And not a sorrow
    Hang any tear on your eyelashes;
    Lie still and deep,
    Sad soul, until the sea-wave washes
The rim o' the sun to-morrow,
    In eastern sky.

But wilt thou cure thine heart
Of love and all its smart,
    Then die, dear, die;
'Tis deeper, sweeter,
    Than on a rose bank to lie dreaming
    With folded eye;
    And then alone, amid the beaming

Of love's stars, thou'lt meet her
    In eastern sky.

Knight. These rites completed, say your further
    pleasure.
Duke. To horse and homewards in all haste : my
    business
Urges each hour. This body bury here,
With all due honours. I myself will build
A monument, whereon, in after times,
Those of his blood shall read his valiant deeds,
And see the image of the bodily nature
He was a man in. Scarcely dare I, lady,
Mock you with any word of consolation :
But soothing care, and silence o'er that sorrow,
Which thine own tears alone may tell to thee
Or offer comfort for; and in all matters
What thy will best desires, I promise thee.
Wilt thou hence with us ?
Sibyl.   Whither you will lead me.
My will lies there, my hope, and all my life
Which was in this world. Yet if I shed tear,
It is not for his death, but for my life.
Dead is he ? Say not so, but that he is
No more excepted from Eternity.
If he were dead I should indeed despair.
Can Wolfram die ? Ay, as the sun doth set :
It is the earth that falls away from light;

Fixed in the heavens, although unseen by us,
The immortal life and light remains triumphant.
And therefore you shall never see me wail,
Or drop base waters of an ebbing sorrow;
No wringing hands, no sighings, no despair,
No mourning weeds will I betake me to;
But keep my thought of him that is no more,
As secret as great nature keeps his soul,
From all the world; and consecrate my being
To that divinest hope, which none can know of
Who have not laid their dearest in the grave.
Farewell, my love,—I will not say to thee
Pale corpse,—we do not part for many days.
A little sleep, a little waking more,
And then we are together out of life.
    Duke. Cover the coffin up. This cold, calm stare
Upon familiar features is most dreadful:
Methinks too the expression of the face
Is changed, since all was settled gently there;
And threatens now. But I have sworn to speak
And think of that no more, which has been done—
Now then into the bustle of the world!
We'll rub our cares smooth there.
    Knight.   This gate, my lord;
There stand the horses.
    Duke.   Then we're mounted straight.
But, pri'thee friend, forget not that the Duke
Is still in prison: I am a poor pilgrim.   [*Exeunt.*

Enter ISBRAND *and* SIEGFRIED *attended.*

Isbr. Dead and gone! a scurvy burthen to this ballad of life. There lies he, Siegfried; my brother, mark
you; and I weep not, nor gnash the teeth, nor curse :
and why not, Siegfried? Do you see this? So should
every honest man be : cold, dead, and leaden-coffined.
This was one who would be constant in friendship, and
the pole wanders : one who would be immortal, and the
light that shines upon his pale forehead now, through
yonder gewgaw window, undulated from its star hundreds of years ago. That is constancy, that is life.
O moral nature!

Siegfr. 'Tis well that you are reconciled to his lot
and your own.

Isbr. Reconciled! A word out of a love tale, that's
not in my language. No, no. I am patient and still
and laborious, a good contented man ; peaceable as an
ass chewing a thistle; and my thistle is revenge. I
do but whisper it now : but hereafter I will thunder
the word, and I shall shoot up gigantic out of this pis-
mire shape, and hurl the bolt of that revenge.

Siegfr. To the purpose : the priests return to complete the burial.

Isbr. Right: we are men of business here. Away
with the body, gently and silently ; it must be buried
in my duke's chapel in Silesia : why, hereafter. (*The
body is borne out by attendants*) That way, fellows :

the hearse stands at the corner of the square: but
reverently, 'tis my brother you carry. [*Exeunt.*

SCENE II.

*A hall in the ducal castle of Munsterberg in the town
of Grüssau in Silesia.* THORWALD, ADALMAR,
ATHULF, ISBRAND, SIEGFRIED; *the* DUKE, *disguised as a pilgrim;* AMALA; *and other ladies
and knights; conversing in various groups.*

Athulf. A fair and bright assembly: never strode
Old arched Grüssau over such a tide
Of helmed chivalry, as when to-day
Our tourney guests swept, leaping billow-like,
Its palace-banked streets. Knights shut in steel,
Whose shields, like water, glassed the soul-eyed
    maidens,
That softly did attend their armed tread,
Flower-cinctured on the temples, whence gushed down
A full libation of star-numbered tresses,
Hallowing the neck unto love's silent kiss,
Veiling its innocent white: and then came squires,
And those who bore war's silken tapestries,
And chequered heralds: 'twas a human river,
Brimful and beating as if the great god,

Who lay beneath it, would arise.　So sways
Time's sea, which Age snows into and makes deep,
When, from the rocky side of the dim future,
Leaps into it a mighty destiny,
Whose being to endow great souls have been
Centuries hoarded, and the world meanwhile
Sate like a beggar upon Heaven's threshold,
Muttering its wrongs.

Siegfr.　　　My sprightly Athulf,
Is it possible that you can waste the day,
Which throws these pillared shades among such beau-
　　ties,
In lonely thought?

Athulf.　　　Why I have left my cup,
A lady's lips, dropping with endless kisses,
Because your minstrels hushed their harps.　Why did
　　they?
This music, which they tickle from the strings,
Is excellent for drowning ears that gape,
When one has need of whispers.

Siegfr.　　　The old governor
Would have it so : his morning nap being o'er,
He's no more need of music, but is moving
Straight to the lists.

Athulf.　　　A curse on that mock war !
How it will shake and sour the blood, that now
Is quiet in the men !　And there's my brother,
Whose sword's his pleasure.　A mere savage man,

Made for the monstrous times, but left out then,
Born by mistake with us.

Adalm. (*to Isbrand*)   Be sure 'tis heavy.
One lance of mine a wolf shut his jaws on
But cracked it not, you'll see his bite upon it:
It lies among the hunting weapons.

   Isbr.   Ay,
With it I saw you once scratch out of life
A blotted Moor.

   Adalm.   The same; it poises well,
And falls right heavy: find it.   [*Exit* ISBRAND.

   Siegfr.   For the tilt,
My brave lord Adalmar?

   Athulf.   What need of asking?
You know the man is sore upon a couch;
But upright, on his bloody-hoofed steed
Galloping o'er the ruins of his foes,
Whose earthquake he hath been, then will he shout,
Laugh, run his tongue along his trembling lip,
And swear his heart tastes honey.

   Siegfr.   Nay, thou'rt harsh;
He was the axe of Mars; but, Troy being felled,
Peace trims her bower with him.

   Athulf.   Ay; in her hand
He's iron still.

   Adalm.   I care not, brother Athulf,
Whether you're right or wrong: 'tis very certain,
Thank God for it, I am not Peace's lap-dog,

But Battle's shaggy whelp. Perhaps, even soon,
Good friend of Bacchus and the rose, you'll feel
Your budding wall of dalliance shake behind you,
And need my spear to prop it.

 Athulf.   Come the time!
You'll see that in our veins runs brother's blood.

 A Lady. Is Siegfried here? At last! I've sought
   . for you
By every harp and every lady's shoulder,
Not ever thinking you could breathe the air
That ducal cub of Munsterberg makes frightful
With his loud talk.

 Siegfr.   Happy in my error,
If thus to be corrected.

Re-enter ISBRAND.

 Isbr.   The lance, my lord:
A delicate tool to breathe a heathen's vein with.

 The Lady. What, Isbrand, thou a soldier? Fie
   upon thee!
Is this a weapon for a fool?

 Isbr. Madam, I pray thee pardon us. The fair have
wrested the tongue from us, and we must give our
speeches a tongue of some metal—steel or gold. And
I beseech thee, lady, call me fool no more: I grow
old, and in old age you know what men become. We
are at court, and there it were sin to call a thing by its
right name : therefore call me a fool no longer, for my

wisdom is on the wane, and I am almost as sententious
as the governor.

The Lady. Excellent: wilt thou become court-con-
fessor?

Isbr. Ay, if thou wilt begin with thy secrets, lady.
But my fair mistress, and you, noble brethren, I pray
you gather around me. I will now speak a word in
earnest, and hereafter jest with you no more: for I
lay down my profession of folly. Why should I wear
bells to ring the changes of your follies on? Doth the
besonneted moon wear bells, she that is the parasite and
zany of the stars, and your queen, ye apes of madness?
As I live I grow ashamed of the duality of my legs,
for they and the apparel, forked or furbelowed, upon
them constitute humanity; the brain no longer: and
I wish I were an honest fellow of four shins when I
look into the note-book of your absurdities. I will ab-
dicate.

The Lady. Brave! but how dispose of your domi-
nions, most magnanimous zany?

Isbr. My heirs at law are manifold. Yonder minister shall have my jacket; he needs many colours
for his deeds. You shall inherit my mantle; for your
sins, (be it whispered,) chatter with the teeth for cold;
and charity, which should be their great-coat, you have
not in the heart.

The Lady. Gramercy: but may I not beg your
coxcomb for a friend?

Isbr. The brothers have an equal claim to that crest :
they may tilt for it.   But now for my crown.   O cap
and bells, ye eternal emblems, hieroglyphics of man's
supreme right in nature; O ye, that only fall on the
deserving, while oak, palm, laurel, and bay rankle on
their foreheads, whose deserts are oft more payable at
the other extremity : who shall be honoured with you ?
Come candidates, the cap and bells are empty.

The Lady. Those you should send to England, for
the bad poets and the critics who praise them.

Isbr. Albeit worthy, those merry men cannot this
once obtain the prize.   I will yield Death the crown
of folly.   He hath no hair, and in this weather might
catch cold and die: besides he has killed the best
knight I knew, Sir Wolfram, and deserves it.   Let
him wear the cap, let him toll the bells; he shall be
our new court-fool: and, when the world is old and
dead, the thin wit shall find the angel's record of man's
works and deeds, and write with a lipless grin on the
innocent first page for a title, ' Here begins Death's
Jest-book.'—There, you have my testament: henceforth speak solemnly to me, and I will give a measured
answer, having relapsed into court-wisdom again.

The Lady. How the wild jester would frighten us !
        Come, Siegfried :
Some of us in a corner wait your music,
Your news, and stories.   My lord Adalmar,
You must be very weary all this time,

The rest are so delighted.   Come along, [*to Siegfr.*
Or else his answer stuns me.

   Adalm.   Joyous creature !
Whose life's first leaf is hardly yet uncurled.

    Athulf. Use your trade's language ; were I journey-
      man
To Mars, the glorious butcher, I would say
She's sleek, and sacrificial flowers would look well
On her white front.

   Adalm.   Now, brother, can you think,
Stern as I am above, that in my depth
There is no cleft wherein such thoughts are hived
As from dear looks and words come back to me,
Storing that honey, love.   O! love I do,
Through every atom of my being.

    Athulf.   Ay,
So do we young ones all.   In winter time
This god of butterflies, this Cupid sleeps,
As they do in their cases ; but May comes ;
With it the bee and he : each spring of mine
He sends me a new arrow, thank the boy.
A week ago he shot me for this year ;
The shaft is in my stomach, and so large
There's scarcely room for dinner.

   Adalm.   Shall I believe thee,
Or judge mortality by this stout sample
I screw my mail o'er ?   Well, it may be so ;
You are an adept in these chamber passions,

And have a heart that's Cupid's arrow cushion
Worn out with use.   I never knew before
The meaning of this love.   But one has taught me,
It is a heaven wandering among men,
The spirit of gone Eden haunting earth.
Life's joys, death's pangs are viewless from its bosom,
Which they who keep are gods : there's no paradise,
There is no heaven, no angels, no blessed spirits,
No souls, or they have no eternity,
If this be not a part of them.
    Athulf.   This in a Court !
Such sort of love might Hercules have felt
Warm from the Hydra fight, when he had fattened
On a fresh slain Bucentaur, roasted whole,
The heart of his pot-belly, till it ticked
Like a cathedral clock.   But in good faith
Is this the very truth ?   Then have I found
My fellow fool.   For I am wounded too
E'en to the quick and inmost, Adalmar.
So fair a creature ! of such charms compact
As nature stints elsewhere ; which you may find
Under the tender eyelid of a serpent,
Or in the gurge of a kiss-coloured rose,
By drops and sparks : but when she moves, you see,
Like water from a crystal overfilled,
Fresh beauty tremble out of her and lave
Her fair sides to the ground.   Of other women,
(And we have beauteous in this court of ours,)

E

I can remember whether nature touched
Their eye with brown or azure, where a vein
Runs o'er a sleeping eyelid, like some streak
In a young blossom; every grace count up,
Here the round turn and crevice of the arm,
There the tress-bunches, or the slender hand
Seen between harpstrings gathering music from them:
But where she is, I'm lost in her abundance,
And when she leaves me I know nothing more,
(Like one from whose awakening temples rolls
The cloudy vision of a god away,)
Than that she was divine.

  Adalm. Fie sir, these are the spiced sighs of a heart,
That bubbles under wine; utter rhyme-gilding,
Beneath man's sober use. What do you speak of?

  Athulf. A woman most divine, and that I love
As you dare never.

  Adalm.   Boy, a truce with talk.
Such words are sacred, placed within man's reach
To be used seldom, solemnly, when speaking
Of what both God and man might overhear,
You unabashed.

  Athulf.   Of what? What is more worthy
Than the delight of youth, being so rare,
Precious, short-lived, and irrecoverable?

  Adalm. When you do mention that adored land,
Which gives you life, pride, and security,
And holy rights of freedom; or in the praise

Of those great virtues and heroic men,
That glorify the earth and give it beams,
Then to be lifted by the like devotion
Would not disgrace God's angels.

    Athulf.   Well sir, laud,
Worship, and swear by them, your native country
And virtues past; a phantom and a corpse:
Such airy stuff may please you.   My desires
Are hot and hungry; they will have their fill
Of living dalliance, gazes, and lip-touches,
Or eat their master.   Now, no more rebuking:
Peace be between us.   For why are we brothers,
Being the creatures of two different gods,
But that we may not be each other's murderers?

    Adalm.   So be it then!   But mark me, brother
        Athulf,
I spoke not from a cold unnatural spirit,
Barren of tenderness.   I feel and know
Of woman's dignity; how it doth merit
Our total being, has all mine this moment:
But they should share with us our level lives:
Moments there are, and one is now at hand,
Too high for them.   When all the world is stirred
By some preluding whisper of that trumpet,
Which shall awake the dead, to do great things,
Then the sublimity of my affection,
The very height of my beloved, shows me
How far above her's glory.   When you've earned

This knowledge, tell me : I will say, you love
As a man should.   [*He retires.*

   Athulf.   But this is somewhat true.
I almost think that I could feel the same
For her. For *her ?* By heavens 'tis Amala,
Amala only, that he so can love.
There ? by her side ? in conference ! at smiles !
Then I am born to be a fratricide.
I feel as I were killing him. Tush, tush ;
A phantom of my passion ! But, if true—
What ? What, my heart ? A strangely-quiet thought,
That will not be pronounced, doth answer me.

(THORWALD *comes forward, attended by the company.*)

   Thorw. Break up ! The day's of age. Knights to
    the lists,
And ladies to look on. We'll break some lances
Before 'tis evening. To your sports, I pray ;
I follow quickly. [*He is left alone with the* DUKE.
    Pilgrim, now your news :
Whence come you ?
   Duke.   Straightway from the holy land,
Whose sanctity such floods of human blood,
Unnatural rain for it, will soon wash out.
   Thorw. You saw our Duke ?
   Duke.   I did : but Melveric
Is strangely altered. When we saw him leap,

Shut up in iron, on his burning steed
From Grüssau's threshold, he had fifty years
Upon his head, and bore them straight and upright,
Through dance, and feast, and knightly tournament.

Thorw. How! Is he not the same? 'Tis but three
    years
And a fourth's quarter past. What is the change?
A silvering of the hair? a deeper wrinkle
On cheek and forehead?

Duke.   I do not think you'd know him,
Stood he where I do. No. I saw him lying
Beside a fountain on a battle-evening:
The sun was setting over the heaped plain;
And to my musing fancy his front's furrows,
With light between them, seemed the grated shadow
Thrown by the ribs of that field's giant, Death;
'Twixt which the finger of the hour did write
‘ This is the grave's.’

Thorw.   How? Looked he sorrowful?
Knows he the dukedom's state?

Duke. (*giving letters to Thorwald*) Ask these.
    He's heard
The tidings that afflict the souls of fathers;
How these two sons of his unfilially
Have vaulted to the saddle of the people,
And charge against him. How he gained the news,
You must know best: what countermine he digs,
Those letters tell your eyes. He bade me say,

His dukedom is his body, and, he forth,
That may be sleeping, but the touch of wrong,
The murderer's barefoot tread will bring him back
Out of his Eastern visions, ere this earth
Has swung the city's length.

    Thorw.   I read as much :
He bids me not to move; no eye to open,
But to sit still and doze, and warm my feet
At their eruption. This security
Is most unlike him. I remember oft,
When the thin harvests shed their withered grain,
And empty poverty yelped sour-mouthed at him,
How he would cloud his majesty of form
With priestly hangings, or the tattered garb
Of the step-seated beggar, and go round
To catch the tavern talk and the street ballad,
And whispers of ancestral prophecies,
Until he knew the very nick of time,
When his heart's arrow would be on the string ;
And, seizing Treason by the arm, would pour
Death back upon him.

    Duke.   He is wary still,
And has a snake's eye under every grass.
Your business is obedience unto him,
Who is your natal star; and mine, to worm,
Leaf after leaf, into the secret volume
Of their designs. Already has our slave,
The grape juice, left the side-door of the youngest

,Open to me.   You think him innocent.
Fire flashes from him ; whether it be such
As treason would consult by, or the coals
Love boils his veins on, shall through this small crevice,
Through which the vine has thrust its cunning tendril,
Be looked and listened for.
    Thorw.   Can I believe it ?
Did not I know him and his spirit's course,
Well as the shape and colour of the sun,
· And when it sets and rises ?   Is this he ?
No : 'tis the shadow of this pilgrim false,
Who stands up in his height of villany,
Shadowy as a hill, and throws his hues
Of contradiction to the heavenly light,
The stronger as it shines upon him most.
Ho ! pilgrim, I have weighed and found thee villain.
Are thy knees used to kneeling ?   It may chance
That thou wilt change the altar for the block :
Prove thou'rt his messenger.
    Duke.   I wait your questions.
The very inmost secret of his heart,
Confided to you, challenge from me.
    Thorw.   First,
A lighter trial.   If you come from him,
Tell me what friend he spoke of most.
    Duke.   Of thee.
    Thorw. Another yet ;
A knight ?

Duke.   There is no living knight his friend.

Thorw. O ill guessed, palmer ! One, whom Melveric
Would give his life, all but his virtue for,
Lived he no more, to raise him from the dead.

 Duke. Right; he would give his soul; Thorwald,
  his soul :—
Friendship is in its depth, and secrets sometimes
Like to a grave.—So loved the Duke that warrior.

 Thorw. Enough, his name ;—the name ?

 Duke.   Ay, ay, *the name*—
Methinks there's nothing in the world but names :
All things are dead; friendship at least I'll blot
From my vocabulary. The man was called—
The knight—I cannot utter't—the knight's name—
Why dost thou ask me ? I know nothing of him.
I have not seen or heard of him, of—Well,
I'll speak of him to no man more—

 Thorw.   Tremble then
When thou dost hear of—Wolfram ! thou art pale :
Confess, or to the dungeon—

 Duke.   Pause ! I am stuffed
With an o'erwhelming spirit : press not thou,
Or I shall burst asunder, and let through
The deluging presence of thy duke. Prepare :
He's near at hand.

 Thorw.   Forbid it, Providence !
He steps on a plot's spring, whose teeth encircle
The throne and city.

Duke. (*disrobing*)   Fear not.   On he comes,
Still as a star robed in eclipse, until
The earthy shadow slips away.   Who rises?
I'm changing: now who am I?
 Thorw.   Melveric!
Munsterberg, as I live and love thee!
 Duke.   Hush!
Is there not danger?
 Thorw.   Ay: we walk on ice
Over the mouth of Hell: an inch beneath us,
Dragon Rebellion lies ready to wake.
Ha! and behold him.

Enter ADALMAR.

 Adalm. Lord Governor, our games are waiting for
  you.
Will you come with me?   Base and muffled stranger,
What dost thou here?   Away.
 Duke.   Prince Adalmar,
Where shall you see me?   I will come again,
This or the next world.   Thou, who carriest
The seeds of a new world, may'st understand me.
Look for me ever.   There's no crack without me
In earth and all around it.   Governor,
Let all things happen, as they will.   Farewell:
Tremble for no one.
 Adalm.   Hence!   The begging monk
Prates emptily.

. *Duke.*   Believe him.

  Thorw.   Well, lead on ;

Wert thou a king, I would not more obey thee.

                          [*Exit with* ADALMAR.

  Duke. Rebellion, treason, parricidal daggers !

This is the bark of the court dogs, that come

Welcoming home their master. My sons too,

Even my sons ! O not sons, but contracts,

Between my lust and a destroying fiend,

Written in my dearest blood, whose date run out,

They are become death-warrants. Parricide,

And Murder of the heart that loved and nourished,

Be merry, ye rich fiends ! Piety's dead,

And the world left a legacy to you.

Under the green-sod are your coffins packed,

So thick they break each other. The days come

When scarce a lover, for his maiden's hair,

Can pluck a stalk whose rose draws not its hue

Out of a hate-killed heart. Nature's polluted,

There's man in every secret corner of her,

Doing damned wicked deeds. Thou art old, world,

A hoary atheistic murderous star :

I wish that thou would'st die, or could'st be slain,

Hell-hearted bastard of the sun.

O that the twenty coming years were over !

Then should I be at rest, where ruined arches

Shut out the troublesome unghostly day ;

And idlers might be sitting on my tomb,

Telling how I did die. How shall I die?
Fighting my sons for power; or of dotage,
Sleeping in purple pressed from filial veins;
To let my epitaph be, " Here lies he,
Who murdered his two children?" Hence cursed
        thought!
I will enquire the purpose of their plot:
There may be good in it, and, if there be,
I'll be a traitor too.   [*Exit.*

SCENE III.

A retired gallery in the ducal castle.

Enter ISBRAND *and* SIEGFRIED.

Isbr. Now see you how this dragon egg of ours
Swells with its ripening plot? Methinks I hear
Snaky rebellion turning restless in it,
And with its horny jaws scraping away
The shell that hides it. All is ready now:
I hold the latch-string of a new world's wicket;
One pull and it rolls in. Bid all our friends
Meet in that ruinous church-yard once again,
By moonrise: until then I'll hide myself;
For these sweet thoughts rise dimpling to my lips,
And break the dark stagnation of my features,
Like sugar melting in a glass of poison.

To-morrow, Siegfried, shalt. thou see me sitting
One of the drivers of this racing earth,
With Grüssau's reins between my fingers.   Ha!
Never since Hell laughed at the church, blood-drunke
From rack and wheel, has there been joy so mad
As that which stings my marrow now.

  Siegfr.   Good cause
The sun-glance of a coming crown to heat you,
And give your thoughts gay colours in the steam
Of a fermenting brain.

  Isbr.   Not alone that.
A sceptre is smooth handling, it is true,
And one grows fat and jolly in a chair
That has a kingdom crouching under it,
With one's name on its collar, like a dog,
To fetch and carry.   But the heart I have
Is a strange little snake.   He drinks not wine,
When he'd be drunk, but poison: he doth fatten
On bitter hate, not love.   And, O that duke!
My life is hate of him; and, when I tread
His neck into the grave, I shall, methinks,
Fall into ashes with the mighty joy,
Or be transformed into a winged star:
That will be all eternal heaven distilled
Down to one thick rich minute.   This sounds madl'
But I am mad when I remember him:
Siegfried, you know not why.

  Siegfr.   I never knew

That you had quarrelled.

Isbr.   True: but did you see
My brother's corpse? There was a wound on't, Sieg-
        fried;
He died not gently, nor in a ripe age;
And I'll be sworn it was the duke that did it,
Else he had not remained in that far land,
And sent his knights to us again.

Siegfr.   I thought
He was the duke's close friend.

Isbr.   Close as his blood:
A double-bodied soul they did appear,
Rather than fellow hearts.

Siegfr.   I've heard it told
That they did swear and write in their best blood,
And her's they loved the most, that who died first
Should, on death's holidays, revisit him
Who still dwelt in the flesh.

Isbr.   O that such bond
Would move the jailor of the grave to open
Life's gate again unto my buried brother,
But half an hour! Were I buried, like him,
There in the very garrets of death's town,
But six feet under earth, (that's the grave's sky,)
I'd jump up into life. But he's a quiet ghost;
He walks not in the churchyard after dew,
But gets to his grave betimes, burning no glow-worms,
Sees that his bones are right, and stints his worms

Most miserly. If you were murdered, Siegfried,
As he was by this duke, should it be so?

   Siegfr. Here speaks again your passion: what
     know we
Of death's commandments to his subject-spirits,
Who are as yet the body's citizens?
What seas unnavigable, what wild forests,
What castles, and what ramparts there may hedge
His icy frontier?

   Isbr.   Tower and roll what may,
There have been goblins bold who have stolen pass-
     ports,
Or sailed the sea, or leaped the wall, or flung
The drawbridge down, and travelled back again.
So would my soul have done. But let it be.
At the doom-twilight shall the ducal cut-throat
Wake by a tomb-fellow he little dreamt of.
Methinks I see them rising with mixed bones,
A pair of patch-work angels.

   Siegfr.   What does this mean?

   Isbr. A pretty piece of kidnapping, that's all.
When Melveric's heart's heart, his new-wed wife,
Upon the bed whereon she bore these sons,
Died, as a blossom does whose inmost fruit
Tears it in twain, and in its stead remains
A bitter poison-berry: when she died,
What her soul left was by her husband laid
In the marriage grave, whereto he doth consign

Himself being dead.

Siegfr.   Like a true loving mate.
Is not her tomb 'mid the cathedral ruins,
Where we to-night assemble?

Isbr.   Say not her's :
A changeling lies there. By black night came I,
And, while a man might change two goblet's liquors,
I laid the lips of their two graves together,
And poured my brother into hers ; while she,
Being the lightest, floated and ran over.
Now lies the murdered where the loved should be ;
And Melveric the dead shall dream of heaven,
Embracing his damnation. There's revenge.
But hush ! here comes one of my dogs, the princes ;
To work with you.   [*Exit Siegfried.*
                    Now for another shape ;
For Isbrand is the handle of the chisels
Which Fate, the turner of men's lives, doth use
Upon the wheeling world.

Enter ATHULF.

                    There is a passion
Lighting his cheek, as red as brother's hate :
If it be so, these pillars shall go down,
Shivering each other, and their ruins be
My step into a dukedom. Doth he speak ?

    Athulf. Then all the minutes of my life to come
Are sands of a great desart, into which

I'm banished broken-hearted. Amala,
I must think thee a lovely-faced murderess,
With eyes as dark and poisonous as nightshade;
Yet no, not so; if thou hadst murdered me,
It had been charitable. Thou hast slain
The love of thee, that lived in my soul's palace
And made it holy: now 'tis desolate,
And devils of abandonment will haunt it,
And call in Sins to come, and drink with them
Out of my heart. But now farewell, my love;
For thy rare sake I could have been a man
One story under god. Gone, gone art thou.
Great and voluptuous Sin now seize upon me,
Thou paramour of Hell's fire-crowned king,
That showedst the tremulous fairness of thy bosom
In heaven, and so didst ravish the best angels.
Come, pour thy spirit all about my soul,
And let a glory of thy bright desires
Play round about my temples. So may I
Be thy knight and Hell's saint for evermore.
Kiss me with fire: I'm thine.

  Isbr.   Doth it run so?
A bold beginning: we must keep him up to't.
  Athulf. Isbrand!
  Isbr.   My prince.
  Athulf.   Come to me. Thou'rt a man
I must know more of. There is something in thee,
The deeper one doth venture in thy being,

That drags us on and down. What dost thou lead to?
Art thou a current to some unknown sea
Islanded richly, full of syren songs
And unknown bliss? Art thou the snaky opening
Of a dark cavern, where one may converse
With night's dear spirits? If thou'rt one of these,
Let me descend thee.

   Isbr.   You put questions to me
In an Egyptian or old magic tongue,
Which I can ill interpret.

   Athulf.   Passion's hieroglyphics;
Painted upon the minutes by mad thoughts,
Dungeoned in misery. Isbrand, answer me;
Art honest, or a man of many deeds
And many faces to them? Thou'rt a plotter,
A politician. Say, if there should come
A fellow, with his being just abandoned
By old desires and hopes, who would do much,—
And who doth much upon this grave-paved star,
In doing, must sin much,—would quick and straight,
Sword-straight and poison-quick, have done with doing;
Would you befriend him?

   Isbr.   I can lend an arm
To good bold purpose. But you know me not,
And I will not be known before my hour.
Why come you here wishing to raise the devil,
And ask me how? Where are your sacrifices?
Eye-water is not his libation, prayers

F

Reach him not through earth's chinks. Bold deeds
  and thoughts,
What men call crimes, are his loved litany;
And from all such good angels keep us! Now sir,
What makes you fretful?
  Athulf.   I have lost that hope,
For which alone I lived. Henceforth my days
Are purposeless; there is no reason further
Why I should be, or should let others be;
No motive more for virtue, for forbearance,
Or anything that's good. The hourly need,
And the base bodily cravings, must be now
The aim of this deserted human engine.
Good may be in this world, but not for me;
Gentle and noble hearts, but not for me;
And happiness, and heroism, and glory,
And love, but none for me. Let me then wander
Amid their banquets, funerals, and weddings,
Like one whose living spirit is Death's Angel.
  Isbr. What? You have lost your love and so turned
  sour?
And who has ta'en your chair in Amala's heaven?
  Athulf. My brother, my Cain; Adalmar.
  Isbr.   I'll help thee, prince:
When will they marry?
  Athulf. I could not wish him in my rage to die
Sooner: one night I'd give him to dream hells.
To-morrow, Isbrand.

Isbr.   Sudden, by my life.
But, out of the black interval, we'll cast
Something upon the moment of their joy,
Which, should it fail to blot, shall so deform it,
That they must write it further down in time.
    Athulf. Let it be crossed with red.
    Isbr.   Trust but to me:
I'll get you bliss. But I am of a sort
Not given to affections. Sire and mother
And sister I had never, and so feel not
Why sin 'gainst them should count so doubly wicked,
This side o' th' sun. If you would wound your foe,
Get swords that pierce the mind: a bodily slice
Is cured by surgeon's butter: let true hate
Leap the flesh wall, or fling his fiery deeds
Into the soul. So he can marry, Athulf,
And then—
    Athulf. Peace, wicked-hearted slave!
Darest thou tempt me? I called on thee for service,
But thou wouldst set me at a hellish work,
To cut my own damnation out of Lust:
Thou'ldst sell me to the fiend. Thou and thy master,
That sooty beast the devil, shall be my dogs,
My curs to kick and beat when I would have you.
I will not bow, nor follow at his bidding,
For his hell-throne. No: I will have a god
To serve my purpose: Hatred be his name;
But 'tis a god, divine in wickedness,

Whom I will worship.   [*Exit.*

Isbr. Then go where Pride and Madness carry thee ;
And let that feasted fatness pine and shrink,
Till thy ghost's pinched in the tight love-lean body.
I see his life, as in a map of rivers,
Through shadows, over rocks, breaking its way,
Until it meet his brother's, and with that
Wrestle and tumble o'er a perilous rock,
Bare as Death's shoulder: one of them is lost,
And a dark haunted flood creeps deadly on
Into the wailing Styx.   Poor Amala !
A thorny rose thy life is, plucked in the dew,
And pitilessly woven with these snakes
Into a garland for the King of the grave.   [*Exit.*

ACT III.

SCENE I.

An apartment in the ducal castle.

The DUKE *and* THORWALD.

Duke. LET them be married: give to Adalmar
The sweet society of woman's soul,
As we impregnate damask swords with odour
Pressed from young flowers' bosoms, so to sweeten
And purify war's lightning.   For the other,
Who catches love by eyes, the court has stars,
That will take up in his tempestuous bosom
The shining place she leaves.
    Thorw.   It shall be done:
The bell, that will ring merrily for their bridal,
Has but few hours to score first.
    Duke.   Good.   I have seen too
Our ripe rebellion's ringleaders.   They meet
By moonrise; with them I: to-night will be
Fiends' jubilee, with heaven's spy among them.
What else was't that you asked?
    Thorw. The melancholy lady you brought with you?
    Duke. Thorwald, I fear her's is a broken heart.

When first I met her in the Egyptian prison,
She was the rosy morning of a woman;
Beauty was rising, but the starry grace
Of a calm childhood might be seen in her.
But since the death of Wolfram, who fell there,
Heaven and one single soul only know how,
I have not dared to look upon her sorrow.
 Thorw. Methinks she's too unearthly beautiful.
Old as I am, I cannot look at her,
And hear her voice, that touches the heart's core,
Without a dread that she will fade o' th' instant.
There's too much heaven in her: oft it rises,
And, pouring out about the lovely earth,
Almost dissolves it. She is tender too;
And melancholy is the sweet pale smile,
With which she gently doth reproach her fortune.
 Duke. What ladies tend her?
 Thorw.   My Amala; she will not often see
One of the others.
 Duke.   Too much solitude
Maintains her in this grief. I will look to't
Hereafter; for the present I've enough.
We must not meet again before to-morrow.
 Thorw. I may have something to report . . .
 Duke. Ho! Ziba.

Enter ZIBA.

Ziba.   Lord of my life!

Duke. I bought this man of Afric from an Arab,
Under the shadow of a pyramid,
For many jewels. He hath skill in language;
And knowledge is in him root, flower, and fruit,
A palm with winged imagination in it,
Whose roots stretch even underneath the grave,
And on them hangs a lamp of magic science
In his soul's deepest mine, where folded thoughts
Lie sleeping on the tombs of magi dead:
So said his master when he parted with him.
I know him skilful, faithful: take him with you;
He's fit for many services.
    Thorw.   I'll try him:
Wilt thou be faithful, Moor?
    Ziba.   As soul to body.
    Thorw. Then follow me. Farewell, my noble
        pilgrim.   [*Exeunt* THORWALD *and* ZIBA.
Duke. It was a fascination, near to madness,
Which held me subjugated to that maiden.
Why do I now so coldly speak of her,
When there is nought between us? O! there is,
A deed as black as the old towers of Hell.
But hence! thou torturing weakness of remorse;
'Tis time when I am dead to think on that:
Yet my sun shines; so courage, heart, cheer up:
Who should be merrier than a secret villain?
                              [*Exit.*

SCENE II.

Another room in the same.

SIBYLLA *and* AMALA.

Sibyl. I would I were a fairy, Amala,
Or knew some of those winged wizard women,
Then I could bring you a more precious gift.
'Tis a wild graceful flower, whose name I know not;
Call it Sibylla's love, while it doth live;
And let it die that you may contradict it,
And say my love doth not, so bears no fruit.
Take it. I wish that happiness may ever
Flow through your days as sweetly and as still,
As did the beauty and the life to this
Out of its roots.
    Amala.   Thanks, my kind Sibylla:
To-morrow I will wear it at my wedding,
Since that must be.
    Sibyl.   Art thou then discontented?
I thought the choice was thine, and Adalmar
A noble warrior worthy of his fortune.
    Amala. O yes: brave, honourable is my bridegroom,
But somewhat cold perhaps. If his wild brother
Had but more constancy and less insolence
In love, he were a man much to my heart.
But, as it is, I must, I will be happy;

And Adalmar deserves that I should love him.
But see how night o'ertakes us.   Good rest, dear :
We will no more profane sleep's stillest hour.
   Sibyl. Good night, then.   [*Exeunt.*

SCENE III.

*A church-yard with the ruins of a spacious gothic
cathedral.   On the cloister walls the* DANCE OF
DEATH *is painted.   On one side the sepulchre of
the Dukes with massy carved folding doors.
Moonlight.*

Enter ISBRAND *and* SIEGFRIED.

   Isbr. Not here?   That wolf-howled, witch-prayed,
         owl-sung fool,
Fat mother moon hath brought the cats their light
A whole thief's hour, and yet they are not met.
I thought the bread and milky thick-spread lies,
With which I plied them, would have drawn to head
The state's bad humours quickly.
   Siegfr.   They delay
Until the twilight strollers are gone home.
   Isbr. That may be.   This is a sweet place methinks :
These arches and their caves, now double-nighted
With heaven's and that creeping darkness, ivy,
Delight me strangely.   Ruined churches oft,
As this, are crime's chief haunt, as ruined angels

Straight become fiends. This tomb too tickleth me
With its wild-rose branches. Dost remember, Siegfried,
About the buried Duchess? In this cradle
I placed the new dead: here the changeling lies.

   Siegfr. Are we so near? A frightful theft!

   Isbr.   Fright! idiot!
Peace; there's a footstep on the pavement.

Enter the DUKE.

                           Welcome!
I thank you, wanderer, for coming first.
They of the town lag still.

   Duke.   The enterprise,
And you its head, much please me.

   Isbr.   You are courteous.

   Duke. Better: I'm honest. But your ways and words
Are so familiar to my memory,
That I could almost think we had been friends
Since our now riper and declining lives
Undid their outer leaves.

   Isbr.   I can remember
No earlier meeting. What need of it? Methinks
We agree well enough: especially
As you have brought bad tidings of the Duke.

   Duke.   If I had time,
And less disturbed thoughts, I'd search my memory
For what thou'rt like. Now we have other matters
To talk about.

Isbr.   And, thank the stingy star-shine,
I see the shades of others of our council.

Enter ADALMAR *and other conspirators.*

'Though late met, well met, friends.   Where stay the
For we're still few here.   [rest?
   Adalm.   They are contented
With all the steps proposed, and keep their chambers
Aloof from the suspecting crowd of eyes,
Which day doth feed with sights for nightly gossip,
Till your hour strikes.
   Isbr.   That's well to keep at home,
And hide, as doth Heaven's wrath, till the last minute.
Little's to say.   We fall as gently on them,
As the first drops of Noah's world-washing shower
Upon the birds' wings and the leaves.   Give each
A copy of this paper: it contains
A quick receipt to make a new creation
In our old dukedom.   Here stands he who framed it.
   Adalm. The unknown pilgrim! You have warrant,
     Isbrand,
For trusting him?
   Isbr.   I have.
   Adalm.   Enough.   How are the citizens?
You feasted them these three days.
   Isbr.   And have them by the heart for't.
'Neath Grüssau's tiles sleep none, whose deepest bosom
My fathom hath not measured; none, whose thoughts

I have not made a map of. In the depth
And labyrinthine home of the still soul,
Where the seen thing is imaged, and the whisper
Joints the expecting spirit, my spies, which are
Suspicion's creeping words, have stolen in,
And, with their eyed feelers, touched and sounded
The little hiding holes of cunning thought,
And each dark crack in which a reptile purpose
Hangs in its chrysalis unripe for birth.
All of each heart I know.

 Duke.   O perilous boast!
Fathom the wavy caverns of all stars,
Know every side of every sand in earth,
And hold in little all the lore of man,
As a dew's drop doth miniature the sun:
But never hope to learn the alphabet,
In which the hieroglyphic human soul
More changeably is painted, than the rainbow
Upon the cloudy pages of a shower,
Whose thunderous hinges a wild wind doth turn.
Know all of each! when each doth shift his thought
More often in a minute, than the air
Dust on a summer path.

 Isbr.   Liquors can lay them:
Grape-juice or vein-juice.

 Duke.   Yet there may be one,
Whose misty mind's perspective still lies hid.

 Isbr. Ha! stranger, where?

Duke. A quiet, listening, flesh-concealed soul.

Isbr. Are the ghosts eaves-dropping? None, that
      do live,
Listen besides ourselves.

> (*A struggle behind: Siegfried drags*
> MARIO *forward.*)

                              Who's there?

Siegfr.   A fellow,
Who crouched behind the bush, dipping his ears
Into the stream of your discourse.

Isbr.   .   Come forward.

Mario. Then lead me. Were it noon, I could not
      find him
Whose voice commands me: in these callous hands
There is as much perception for the light,
As in the depth of my poor dayless eyes.

Isbr.   Thy hand then.

Mario. Art thou leader here?

Isbr.   .   Perchance.

Mario. Then listen, as I listened unto you,
And let my life and story end together,
If it seem good to you. A Roman am I;
A Roman in unroman times: I've slept
At midnight in our Capitolian ruins,
And breathed the ghost of our great ancient world,
Which there doth walk: and among glorious visions,
That the unquiet tombs sent forth to me,
Learned I the love of freedom. Scipio saw I   .

Washing the stains of Carthage from his sword,
And his freed poet, playing on his lyre
A melody men's souls did sing unto:
Oak-bound and laurelled heads, each man a coun
And in the midst, like a sun o'er the sea,
(Each helm in the crowd gilt by a ray from him,
Bald Julius sitting lonely in his car,
Within the circle of whose laurel wreath
All spirits of the earth and sea were spell-bound.
Down with him to the grave! Down with the g
Stab, Cassius; Brutus, through him; through him
Dead.—As he fell there was a tearing sigh:
Earth stood on him; her roots were in his heart;
They fell together. Cæsar and his world
Lie in the Capitol; and Jove lies there,
With all the gods of Rome and of Olympus;
Corpses: and does the eagle batten on them?
No; she is flown: the owl sits in her nest;
The toge is cut for cowls; and falsehood dozes
In the chair of freedom, triple-crowned beast,
King Cerberus. Thence I have come in time
To see one grave for foul oppression dug,
Though I may share it.

 Isbr.   Nay: thou'rt a bold he
Welcome among us.

 Mario. ·   I was guided hither
By one in white, garlanded like a bride,
Divinely beautiful, leading me softly;

And she doth place my hand in thine, once more
Bidding me guard her honour amongst men ;
And so I will, with death to him that soils it :
For she is Liberty.

    Adalm.   In her name we take thee ;
And for her sake welcome thee brotherly.
At the right time thou comest to us, dark man,
Like an eventful unexpected night,
Which finishes a row of plotting days,
Fulfilling their designs.

    Isbr.   Now then, my fellows,
No more ; but to our unsuspected homes.
Good night to all who rest ; hope to the watchful.
Stranger, with me.   [*To Mario.*
                [*Exeunt : manet* DUKE.

    Duke. I'm old and desolate. O were I dead
With thee, my wife ! Oft have I lain by night
Upon thy grave, and burned with the mad wish
To raise thee up to life. Thank God, whom then
I might have thought not pitiful, for lending
No ear to such a prayer. Far better were I
Thy grave-fellow, than thou alive with me,
Amid the fears and perils of the time.

            Enter ZIBA.

Who's in the dark there ?
    Ziba.   One of the dark's colour :
Ziba, thy slave.

Duke.   Come at a wish, my Arab.

Is Thorwald's house asleep yet?

Ziba.   No: his lights still burn.

Duke. Go; fetch a lantern and some working fellows

With spade and pickaxe. Let not Thorwald come.

In good speed do it.   [*Exit* ZIBA.

That alone is left me:

I will abandon this ungrateful country,

And leave my dukedom's earth behind me; all,

Save the small urn that holds my dead beloved:

That relic will I save from my wrecked princedom;

Beside it live and die.

(*Enter* THORWALD, ZIBA, *and gravediggers.*)

Thorwald with them!

Old friend, I hoped you were in pleasant sleep:

'Tis a late walking hour.

Thorw.   I came to learn

Whether the slave spoke true. This haunted hour,

What would you with the earth? Dig you for treasure?

Duke. Ay, I do dig for treasure. To the vault,

Lift up the kneeling marble woman there,

And delve down to the coffin. Ay, for treasure:

The very dross of such a soul and body

Shall stay no longer in this land of hate.

I'll covetously rake the ashes up

Of this my love-consumed incense star,

And in a golden urn, over whose sides
An unborn life of sculpture shall be poured,
They shall stand ever on my chamber altar.
I am not Heaven's rebel; think't not of me;
Nor that I'd trouble her sepulchral sleep
For a light end.   Religiously I come
To change the bed of my beloved lady,
That what remains below of us may join,
Like its immortal.
    Thorw.   There is no ill here:
And yet this breaking through the walls, that sever
The quick and cold, led never yet to good.
    Ziba. Our work is done: betwixt the charmed
        moonshine
And the coffin lies nought but a nettle's shade,
That shakes its head at the deed.
    Duke.   Let the men go.
                    [*Exeunt labourers.*
            Now Death, thou shadowy miser,
I am thy robber; be not merciful,
But take me in requital.   There is she then;
I cannot hold my tears, thinking how altered.
O thoughts, ye fleeting, unsubstantial family!
Thou formless, viewless, and unuttered memory!
How dare ye yet survive that gracious image,
Sculptured about the essence whence ye rose?
That words of her should ever dwell in me,
Who is as if she never had been born

                    G

To all earth's millions, save this one! Nay, prithee,
Let no one comfort me.   I'll mourn awhile
Over her memory.

    Thorw.   Let the past be past,
And Lethe freeze unwept on over it.
What is, be patient with: and, with what shall be,
Silence the body-bursting spirit's yearnings.
Thou say'st that, when she died, that day was spilt
All beauty flesh could hold; that day went down
An oversouled creation.   The time comes
When thou shalt find again thy blessed love,
Pure from all earth, and with the usury
Of her heaven-hoarded charms.

    Duke.   Is this the silence
That I commanded?   Fool, thou say'st a lesson
Out of some philosophic pedant's book.
I loved no desolate soul: she was a woman,
Whose spirit I knew only through those limbs,
Those tender members thou dost dare despise;
By whose exhaustless beauty, infinite love,
Trackless expression only, I did learn
That there was aught yet viewless and eternal;
Since they could come from such alone.   Where is she?
Where shall I ever see her as she was?
With the sweet smile, she smiled only on me;
With those eyes full of thoughts, none else could see?
Where shall I meet that brow and lip with mine?
Hence with thy shadows!   But her warm fair body,

Where's that? There, mouldered to the dust. Old man,
If thou dost dare to mock my ears again
With thy ridiculous, ghostly consolation,
I'll send thee to the blessings thou dost speak of.

    Thorw. For heaven's and her sake restrain this pas-
        sion.

    Duke. She died. But Death is old and half worn out:
Are there no chinks in't? Could she not come to me?
Ghosts have been seen; but never in a dream,
After she'd sighed her last, was she the blessing
Of these desiring eyes. All, save my soul,
And that but for her sake, were his who knew
The spell of Endor, and could raise her up.

    Thorw. Another time that thought were impious.
Unreasonable longings, such as these,
Fit not your age and reason. In sorrow's rage
Thou dost demand and bargain for a dream,
Which children smile at in their tales.

    Ziba.   Smile ignorance!
But, sure as men have died strong necromancy
Hath set the clock of time and nature back;
And made Earth's rooty, ruinous, grave-floored caverns
Throb with the pangs of birth. Ay, were I ever
Where the accused innocent did pray
Acquittal from dead lips, I would essay
My sires' sepulchral magic.

    Duke.   Slave, thou tempt'st me
To lay my sword's point to thy throat, and say

" Do it or die thyself."

Thorw.   Prithee, come in.
To cherish hopes like these is either madness,
Or a sure cause of it.   Come in and sleep:
To morrow we'll talk further.

Duke.   Go in thou.
Sleep blinds no eyes of mine, till I have proved
This slave's temptation.

Thorw.   Then I leave you to him.
Good night again.   [*Exit Thorwald.*

Duke.   Good night, and quiet slumbers.
Now then, thou juggling African, thou shadow,
Think'st thou I will not murder thee this night,
If thou again dare tantalize my soul
With thy accursed hints, thy lying boasts?
Say, shall I stab thee?

Ziba.   Then thou murder'st truth.
I spoke of what I'd do.

Duke.   You told ghost-lies,
And held me for a fool because I wept.
Now, once more, silence: or to-night I shed
Drops royaller and redder than those tears.

Enter ISBRAND *and* SIEGFRIED.

Isbr. Pilgrim, not yet abed? Why, ere you've time
To lay your cloak down, heaven will strip off night,
And show her daily bosom.

Duke.   Sir, my eyes

Never did feel less appetite for sleep:
I and my slave intend to watch till morrow.
  Isbr. Excellent. You're a fellow of my humour.
I never sleep o' nights: the black sky likes me,
And the soul's solitude, while half mankind
Lie quiet in earth's shade and rehearse death.
Come, let's be merry: I have sent for wine,
And here it comes.   [*It is brought in.*
                    These mossy stones about us
Will serve for stools, although they have been turrets,
Which scarce aught touched but sunlight, or the claw
Of the strong-winged eagles, who lived here
And fed on battle-bones. Come sit, sir stranger;
Sit too, my devil-coloured one; here's room
Upon my rock. Fill, Siegfried
  Siegfr.   Yellow wine,
And rich be sure. How like you it?
  Duke. Better ne'er wetted lip.
  Isbr. Then fill again. Come, hast no song to-night,
Siegfried? Nor you, my midnight of a man?
I'm weary of dumb toping.
  Siegfr.   Yet you sing not.
My songs are staler than the cuckoo's tune:
And you, companions?
  Duke.   We are quite unused.
  Isbr. Then you shall have a ballad of my making.
  Siegfr. How? do you rhyme too?
  Isbr. Sometimes, in rainy weather.

Here's what I made one night, while picking poisons
To make the rats a sallad.

    Duke.   And what's your tune?

    Isbr. What is the night-bird's tune, wherewith she
      startles
The bee out of his dream, that turns and kisses
The inmost of his flower and sleeps again?
What is the lobster's tune when he is boiling?
I hate your ballads that are made to come
Round like a squirrel's cage, and round again.
We nightingales sing boldly from our hearts:
So listen to us.

Song by Isbrand.

Squats on a toad-stool under a tree
  A bodiless childfull of life in the gloom,
Crying with frog voice, " What shall I be?
Poor unborn ghost, for my mother killed me
  Scarcely alive in her wicked womb.
What shall I be? shall I creep to the egg
  That's cracking asunder yonder by Nile,
      And with eighteen toes,
      And a snuff-taking nose,
  Make an Egyptian crocodile?
Sing, ' Catch a mummy by the leg
      And crunch him with an upper jaw,
      Wagging tail and clenching claw;
      Take a bill-full from my craw,

Neighbour raven, caw, O caw,
    Grunt, my crocky, pretty maw !'

" Swine, shall I be you ? Thou'rt a dear dog ;
    But for a smile, and kiss, and pout,
    I much prefer *your* black-lipped snout,
        Little, gruntless, fairy hog,
        Godson of the hawthorn hedge.
    For, when Ringwood snuffs me out,
        And 'gins my tender paunch to grapple,
        Sing, ' Twixt your ancles visage wedge,
            And roll up like an apple.'

" Serpent Lucifer, how do you do ?
Of your worms and your snakes I'd be one or two ;
    For in this dear planet of wool and of leather
'Tis pleasant to need neither shirt, sleeve, nor shoe,
    And have arm, leg, and belly together.
    Then aches your head, or are you lazy ?
    Sing, ' Round your neck your belly wrap,
    Tail-a-top, and make your cap
        Any bee and daisy.'

" I'll not be a fool, like the nightingale
Who sits up all midnight without any ale,
        Making a noise with his nose ;
Nor a camel, although 'tis a beautiful back :
Nor a duck, notwithstanding the music of quack,

And the webby, mud-patting toes.
I'll be a new bird with the head of an ass,
   Two pigs' feet, two mens' feet, and two of a hen;
Devil-winged; dragon-bellied; grave-jawed, because
    grass
  Is a beard that's soon shaved, and grows seldom again
  Before it is summer; so cow all the rest;
  The new Dodo is finished. O! come to my nest."

Siegfr. A noble hymn to the belly gods indeed:
Would that Pythagoras heard thee, boy!
  Isbr. I fear you flatter: 'tis perhaps a little
Too sweet and tender, but that is the fashion;
Besides my failing is too much sentiment.
Fill the cups up, and pass them round again;
I'm not my nightly self yet. There's creation
In these thick yellow drops. By my faith, Siegfried,
A man of meat and water's a thin beast,
But he who sails upon such waves as these
Begins to be a fellow. The old gods
Were only men and wine.
  Siegfr.   Here's to their memory.
They're dead, poor sinners, all of them but Death,
Who has laughed down Jove's broad, ambrosian brow,
Furrowed with earth-quake frowns: and not a ghost
Haunts the gods' town upon Olympus' peak.
  Isbr. Methinks that earth and heaven are grown bad
    neighbours,

And have blocked up the common door between them.
Five hundred years ago had we sat here
So late and lonely, many a jolly ghost
Would have joined company.

    Siegfr.   To trust in story,
In the old times Death was a feverish sleep,
In which men walked. The other world was cold
And thinly-peopled, so life's emigrants
Came back to mingle with the crowds of earth :
But now great cities are transplanted thither,
Memphis, and Babylon, and either Thebes,
And Priam's towery town with its one beech.
The dead are most and merriest : so be sure
There will be no more haunting, till their towns
Are full to the garret ; then they'll shut their gates,
To keep the living out, and perhaps leave
A dead or two between both kingdoms.

    Duke.   Ziba;
Hear'st thou, phantastic mountebank, what's said ?

    Ziba. Nay : as I live and shall be one myself,
I can command them hither.

    Isbr.   Whom ?

    Ziba.   Departed spirits.

    Duke. He who dares think that words of human
        speech,
A chalky ring with monstrous figures in it,
Or smoky flames can draw the distant souls
Of those, whose bones and monuments are dust,

Must shudder at the restless, broken death,
Which he himself in age shall fall into.

   Isbr. Suppose we four had lived in Cyrus' time,
And had our graves under Egyptian grass,
D'you think, at whistling of a necromant,
I'd leave my wine or subterranean love
To know his bidding? Mummies cannot pull
The breathing to them, when they'd learn the news.

   Ziba. Perhaps they do, in sleep, in swoons, in fevers:
But your belief's not needed.

      [*To the Duke*].   You remember
The damsel dark at Mecca, whom we saw
Weeping the death of a pale summer flower,
Which her spear-slain beloved had tossed to her
Galloping into battle?

   Duke.   ·   Happy one!
Whose eyes could yield a tear to soothe her sorrows.
But what's that to the point?

   Ziba.   As those tears fell,
A magic scholar passed; and, their cause known,
Bade her no longer mourn: he called a bird,
And bade it with its bill select a grain
Out of the gloomy death-bed of the blossom.
The feathery bee obeyed; and scraped aside
The sand, and dropped the seed into its grave:
And there the old plant lay, still and forgotten,
By its just budding grandsons; but not long:
For soon the floral necromant brought forth

A wheel of amber, (such may Clotho use
When she spins lives,) and, as he turned and sung,
The mould was cracked and shouldered up; there came
A curved stalk, and then two leaves unfurled,
And slow and straight between them there arose,
Ghostily still, again the crowned flower.
Is it not easier to raise a man,
Whose soul strives upward ever, than a plant,
Whose very life stands halfway on death's road,
Asleep and buried half?
 Duke.   This was a cheat:
The herb was born anew out of a seed,
Not raised out of a bony skeleton.
What tree is man the seed of?
 Ziba.   Of a ghost;
Of his night-coming, tempest-waved phantom:
And even as there is a round dry grain
In a plant's skeleton, which being buried
Can raise the herb's green body up again;
So is there such in man, a seed-shaped bone,
Aldabaron, called by the Hebrews Luz,
Which, being laid into the ground, will bear
After three thousand years the grass of flesh,
The bloody, soul-possessed weed called man.
 Isbr. Let's have a trick then in all haste, I prithee.
The world's man-crammed; we want no more of them:
But show me, if you will, some four-legged ghost;
Rome's mother, the she-wolf; or the fat goat

From whose dugs Jove sucked godhead ; any thing ;
Pig, bullock, goose ; for they have goblins too,
Else ours would have no dinner.

    Ziba.   Were you worthy,
I'd raise a spirit whom your conscience knows ;
And he would drag thee down into that world,
Whither thou didst send him.

    Isbr.   Thanks for the offer.
Our wine's out, and these clouds, whose blackest wombs
Seem swelling with a second centaur-birth,
Threaten plain water. So good night.

                   [*Exit with Siegfried.*

    Duke. Obstinate slave ! Now that we are alone,
Durst thou again say life and soul has lifted
The dead man from the grave, and sent him walking
Over the earth ?

    Ziba.   I say it, and will add
Deed to my word, not oath. Within what tomb
Dwells he, whom you would call ?

    Duke.   There. But stand off !
If you do juggle with her holy bones,
By God I'll murder thee. I don't believe you,
For here next to my heart I wear a bond,
Written in the blood of one who was my friend,
In which he swears that, dying first, he would
Borrow some night his body from the ground,
To visit me once more. One day we quarrelled,
Swords hung beside us and we drew : he fell.

Yet never has his bond or his revenge
Raised him to my bed-side, haunting his murderer,
Or keeping blood-sealed promise to his friend.
Does not this prove you lie?

 Ziba.   'Tis not my spell:
Shall I try that with him?

 Duke.   No, no! not him.
The heavy world press on him, where he lies,
With all her towers and mountains!

 Ziba.   Listen, lord.
Time was when Death was young and pitiful,
Though callous now by use: and then there dwelt,
In the thin world above, a beauteous Arab,
Unmated yet and boyish. To his couch
At night, which shone so starry through the boughs,
A pale flower-breathed nymph with dewy hair
Would often come, but all her love was silent;
And ne'er by day-light could he gaze upon her,
For ray by ray, as morning came, she paled,
And like a snow of air dissolv'd i' th' light,
Leaving behind a stalk with lilies hung,
Round which her womanish graces had assembled.
So did the early love-time of his youth
Pass with delight: but when, compelled at length,
He left the wilds and woods for riotous camps
And cities full of men, he saw no more,
Tho' prayed and wept for, his old bed-time vision,
The pale dissolving maiden. He would wander

Sleepless about the waste, benighted fields,
Asking the speechless shadows of his thoughts
" Who shared my couch? Who was my love? Where
    is she?"
Thus passing through a grassy burial-ground,
Wherein a new-dug grave gaped wide for food,
" Who was she?" cried he, and the earthy mouth
Did move its nettle-bearded lips together,
And said " 'Twas I—I, Death: behold our child!"
The wanderer looked, and on the lap of the pit
A young child slept as at a mother's breast.
He raised it and he reared it.   From that infant
My race, the death-begotten, draw their blood:
Our prayer for the diseased works more than medicine;
Our blessings oft secure grey hairs and happy
To new-born infants; and, in case of need,
The dead and gone are re-begotten by us,
And motherlessly born to second life.

    Duke. I've heard your tale.   Now exorcise: but,
        mark!
If thou dost dare to make my heart thy fool,
I'll send thee to thy grave-mouthed grandam, Arab.

    Ziba. Wilt thou submit unmurmuring to all evils,
Which this recall to a forgotten being
May cause to thee and thine?

    Duke.   With all my soul,
So I may take the good.

    Ziba.   And art thou ready

To follow, if so be its will, the ghost,
Whom you will re-imbody, to the place
Which it doth now inhabit?
Duke.   My first wish.
Now to your sorcery: and no more conditions,
In hopes I may break off.   All ill be mine,
Which shall the world revisit with the being
That lies within.
Ziba.   Enough.   Upon this scroll
Are written words, which read, even in a whisper,
Would in the air create another star;
And, more than thunder-tongued storms in the sky,
Make the old world to quake and sweat with fear;
And, as the chilly damps of her death-swoon
Fall and condense, they to the moon reflect
The forms and colours of the pale old dead.
Laid there among the bones, and left to burn,
With sacred spices, its keen vaporous power
Would draw to life the earliest dead of all,
Swift as the sun doth ravish a dew-drop
Out of a flower.   But see, the torch-flame dies:
How shall I light it?
Duke.   Here's my useless blood-bond;
These words, that should have waked illumination
Within a corpse's eyes, will make a tinder,
Whose sparks might be of life instead of fire.
Burn it.
Ziba.   An incense for thy senses, god of those,

To whom life is as death to us; who were,
Ere our grey ancestors wrote history;
When these our ruined towers were in the rock;
And our great forests, which do feed the sea
With storm-souled fleets, lay in an acorn's cup:
When all was seed that now is dust; our minute
Invisibly far future. Send thy spirit
From plant of the air, and from the air and earth,
And from earth's worms, and roots, again to gather
The dispersed being, 'mid whose bones I place
The words which, spoken, shall destroy death's king-
    dom,
And which no voice, but thunder, can pronounce.
Marrow fill bone, and vine-like veins run round them,
And flesh, thou grass, mown wert thou long ago,—
Now comes the brown dry after-crop. Ho! ghost!
There's thy old heart a-beating, and thy life
Burning on the old hearth. Come home again!

   Duke. Hush! Do you hear a noise?

   Ziba.   It is the sound
Of the ghost's foot on Jacob's ladder-rungs.

   Duke. More like the tread upon damp stony steps
Out of a dungeon. Dost thou hear a door
Drop its great bolt and grate upon its hinges?

   Ziba. Serpentine Hell! That is thy staircase echo,
                             [*aside.*
And thy jaws' groaning. What betides it?

   Duke. Thou human murder-time of night,

What hast thou done?

Ziba. My task : give me to death, if the air has not
What was the earth's but now. Ho there ! i' th' vault.

A Voice. Who breaks my death ?

Ziba. Draw on thy body, take up thy old limbs,
And then come forth tomb-born.

Duke.   One moment's peace !
Let me remember what a grace she had,
Even in her dying hour : her soul set not,
But at its noon Death like a cloud came o'er it,
And now hath passed away.   O come to me,
Thou dear returned spirit of my wife ;
And, surely as I clasp thee once again,
Thou shalt not die without me.

Ziba.   Ho ! there, Grave,
Is life within thee ?

The Voice.   Melveric, I am here.

Duke. Did'st hear that whisper ?   Open, and let in
The blessing to my eyes, whose subtle breath
Doth penetrate my heart's quick; and let me hear
That dearest name out of those dearest lips.
Who comes back to my heart ?

(MANDRAKE *runs out of the sepulchre.*)

Ziba.   Momus of Hell, what's this ?

Duke. Is this thy wretched jest, thou villanous fool ?
But I will punish thee, by heaven ; and thou too
                                        [*To Mandrake.*

H

Shalt soon be what thou shouldst have better acted.

Mandr. Excuse me: as you have thought proper
to call me to the living, I shall take the liberty of re-
maining alive. If you want to speak to another ghost,
of longer standing, look into the old lumber-room of a
vault again: some one seems to be putting himself together there. Good night, gentlemen, for I must travel
to Egypt once more.   [*Exit.*

Duke. Thou disappointed cheat! Was this a fellow,
Whom thou hadst hired to act a spectral part?
Thou see'st how well he does it. But away!
Or I will teach thee better to rehearse it.

Ziba. Death is a hypocrite then, a white dissembler,
Like all that doth seem good! I am put to shame.
                                             [*Exit.*

Duke. Deceived and disappointed vain desires!
Why laugh I not, and ridicule myself?
'Tis still, and cold, and nothing in the air
But an old grey twilight, or of eve or morn,
I know not which, dim as futurity,
And sad and hoary as the ghostly past,
Fills up the space. Hush! not a wind is there,
Not a cloud sails over the battlements,
Not a bell tolls the hour. Is there an hour?
Or is not all gone by, which here did hive,
Of men and their life's ways? Could I but hear
The ticking of a clock, or some one breathing,
Or e'en a cricket's chirping, or the grating

Of the old gates amidst the marble tombs,
I should be sure that this was still the world.
Hark! Hark! Doth nothing stir?
No light, and still no light, besides this ghost
That mocks the dawn, unaltered? Still no sound?
No voice of man? No cry of beast? No rustle
Of any moving creature? And sure I feel
That I remain the same: no more round blood-drops
Roll joyously along my pulseless veins:
The air I seem to breathe is still the same:
And the great dreadful thought, that now comes o'er me,
Must remain ever as it is, unchanged.—
This moment doth endure for evermore;
Eternity hath overshadowed time;
And I alone am left of all that lived,
Pent in this narrow, horrible conviction.
Ha! the dead soon will wake! My Agnes, rise;
Rise up, my wife! One look, ere Wolfram comes;
Quick, or it is too late: the murdered hasten:
My best-beloved, come once to my heart . .
But ah! who art thou?

                    (*The gates of the sepulchre fly open and
                        discover* WOLFRAM.)

Wolfr.   Wolfram, murderer,
To whose heart thou didst come with horrid purpose.
  Duke. Lie of my eyes, begone! Art thou not dead?
Are not the worms, that ate thy marrow, dead?
What dost thou here, thou wretched goblin fool?

Think'st thou, I fear thee? Thou man-mocking air,
Thou art not truer·than a mirror's image,
Nor half so lasting. Back again to coffin,
Thou baffled idiot spectre, or haunt cradles:
Or stay, and I'll laugh at thee. Guard thyself,
If thou pretendest life.

    Wolfr. Is this thin air, that thrusts thy sword away?
Flesh, bones, and soul, and blood that thou stol'st from
      me,
Upon thy summons, bound by heart-red letters,
Here Wolfram stands: what wouldst thou?

    Duke.   What sorcery else,
But that cursed compact, could have made full Hell
Boil over, and spill thee, thou topmost damned?
But down again! I'll see no more of thee.
Hound to thy kennel, to your coffin bones,
Ghost to thy torture!

    Wolfr.   Thou returnest with me;
So make no hurry. I will stay awhile
To see how the old world goes, feast and be merry,
And then to work again.

    Duke.   Darest thou stand there,
Thou shameless vapour, and assert thyself,
While I defy, and question, and deride thee?
The stars, I see them dying: clearly all
The passage of this night remembrance gives me,
And I think coolly: but my brain is mad,
Else why behold I that? Is't possible

Thou'rt true, and worms have vomited thee up
Upon this rind of earth? No; thou shalt vanish.
Was it for this I hated thee and killed thee?
I'll have thee dead again, and hounds and eagles
Shall be thy graves, since this old, earthy one
Hath spat thee out for poison.

   Wolfr.   Thou, old man,
Art helpless against me. I shall not harm thee;
So lead me home. I am not used to sunlight,
And morn's a-breaking.

   Duke.   Then there is rebellion
Against all kings, even Death. Murder's worn out
And full of holes; I'll never make't the prison,
Of what I hate, again. Come with me, spectre;
If thou wilt live against the body's laws,
Thou murderer of Nature, it shall be
A question, which haunts which, while thou dost last.
So come with me.   [*Exeunt.*

ACT IV.

SCENE I.

An apartment in the Governor's palace.

The DUKE *and an attendant.*

Duke. YOUR lord sleeps yet?

Attend.   An hour ago he rose:
About this time he's busy with his falcons,
And then he takes his meal.

    Duke.   I'll wait for him.

                      [Exit Attendant.

How strange it is that I can live to day;
Nay look like other men, who have been sleeping
On quiet pillows and not dreamt! Methinks
The look of the world's a lie, a face made up
O'er graves and fiery depths ; and nothing's true
But what is horrible. If man could see
The perils and diseases that he elbows,
Each day he walks a mile ; which catch at him,
Which fall behind and graze him as he passes ;
Then would he know that Life's a single pilgrim,
Fighting unarmed amongst a thousand soldiers.
It is this infinite invisible
Which we must learn to know, and yet to scorn,
And, from the scorn of that, regard the world

As from the edge of a far star. Now then
I feel me in the thickest of the battle;
The arrow-shower pours down, swords hew, mines open
Their ravenous mouths about me; it rains death;
But cheerly I defy the braggart storm,
And set my back against a rock, to fight
Till I am bloodily won.

Enter THORWALD.

Thorw.   How? here already?
I'm glad on't, and to see you look so clear.
After that idle talk. How did it end?

Duke. Scarcely as I expected.

Thorw.   Dared he conjure?
But surely you have seen no ghost last night:
You seem to have supped well and slept.

Duke.   We'd wine,
And some wild singing. Of the necromancy
We'll speak no more. Ha! Do you see a shadow?

Thorw. Ay: and the man who casts it.

Duke. Tis true; my eyes are dim and dull with
        watching.
This castle that fell down, and was rebuilt
With the same stones, is the same castle still;
And so with him.

Enter WOLFRAM.

Thorw. What mean you?

Duke.   Impudent goblin!

Darest thou the day-light? Dar'st be seen of more
Than me, the guilty? Vanish! Though thou'rt there,
I'll not believe I see thee. Or is this
The work of necromantic Conscience? Ha!
'Tis nothing but a picture: curtain it.
Strange visions, my good Thorwald, are begotten,
When Sleep o'ershadows waking.

 Thorw.   Who's the stranger?
You speak as one familiar.

 Duke.   Is aught here
Besides our-selves? I think not.

 Thorw.   Yet you gaze
Straight on the man.

 Duke.   A villanous friend of mine;
Of whom I must speak well, and still permit him
To follow me. So thou'rt yet visible,
Thou grave-breaker! If thou wilt haunt me thus,
I'll make thee my fool, ghost, my jest and zany.
'Tis his officious gratitude that pains me:
The carcase owes to me its ruinous life,
(Between whose broken walls and hideous arches
You see the other world's grey spectral light;)
Therefore he clings to me so ivily.
Now, goblin, lie about it. 'Tis in truth
A faithful slave.

 Wolfr.   If I had come unsummoned,
If I had burst into your sunny world,
And stolen visibility and birth

Against thy prayers, thus shouldst thou speak to me :
But thou hast forced me up, remember that.
I am no fiend, no foe; then let me hear
These stern and tyrannous rebukes no more.
Wilt thou be with the born, that have not died ?
I vanish : now a short farewell.   I fade ;
The air doth melt me, and, my form being gone,
I'm all thou see'st not.   [*He disappears.*

Duke. Dissolved like snow in water ! Be my cloud,
My breath, and fellow soul, I can bear all,
As long as thou art viewless to these others.
Now there are two of us.   How stands the bridal ?

Thorw. This evening 'twill be held.

Duke.   Good ; and our plot
Leaps on your pleasure's lap; here comes my gang ;
Away with you.   [*Exit Thorwald.*
I do begin to feel
As if I were a ghost among the men,
As all, whom I loved, are ; for their affections
Hang on things new, young, and unknown to me :
And that I am is but the obstinate will
Of this my hostile body.

Enter ISBRAND, ADALMAR, *and* SIEGFRIED.

Isbr. Come, let's be doing: we have talked whole
      nights
Of what an instant, with one flash of action,
Should have performed : you wise and speaking people

Need some one, with a hatchet-stroke, to free
The Pallas of your Jove-like headaches.

   Duke.   Patience:
Fledging comes after hatching.   One day more:
This evening brings the wedding of the prince,
And with it feasts and maskings.   In mid bowls
And giddy dances let us fall upon them.

   Siegfr. Well thought : our enemies will be as-
      sembled.

   Isbr. I like to see Ruin at dinner time,
Firing his cannons with the match they lit
For the buck-roasting faggots.   But what say you
To what concerns you most?   [*to Adalmar.*

   Adalm.   That I am ready
To hang my hopeful crown of happiness
Upon the temple of the public good.

   Isbr. Of that no need.   Your wedding shall be
      finished;
Or left, like a full goblet yet untasted,
To be drunk up with greater thirst from toil.
I'll wed too when I've time.   My honest pilgrim,
The melancholy lady, you brought with you,
Looks on me with an eye of much content:
I have sent some rhymed love-letters unto her,
In my best style.   D' you think we're well matched?

   Adalm. How? Would you prop the peach upon the
      upas ?

   Isbr. True: I am rough, a surly bellowing storm;

But fallen, never tear did hang more tender
Upon the eye-lash of a love-lorn girl,
Or any Frenchman's long, frost-bitten nose,
Than in the rosecup of that lady's life
I shall lie trembling. Pilgrim, plead for me
With a tongue love-oiled.

 Duke.   Win her, sir, and wear her.
But you and she are scarcely for one world.

 Isbr. Enough; I'll wed her. Siegfried, come with me;
We'll talk about it in the rainy weather.
Pilgrim, anon I find you in the ruins,
Where we had wine last night.

         [Exit with Siegfried.

 Adalm. Would that it all were over, and well over!
Suspicions flash upon me here and there:
But we're in the mid ocean without compass,
Winds wild, and billows rolling us away:
Onwards with hope!

 Duke.   Of what? Youth, is it possible
That thou art toiling here for liberty,
And others' welfare, and such virtuous shadows
As philosophic fools and beggars raise
Out of the world that's gone? Thou'lt sell thy birth-
   right
For incense praise, less tickling to the sense
Than Esau's pottage steam?

 Adalm.   No, not for these,
Fame's breath and praise, its shadow. 'Tis my humour

To do what's right and good.

   Duke.   Thou'rt a strange prince.
Why all the world, except some fifty lean ones,
Would, in your place and at your ardent years,
Seek the delight that lies in woman's limbs
And mountain-covering grapes.   What's to be royal,
Unless you pick those girls, whose cheeks you fancy,
As one would cowslips?   And see hills and valleys
Mantled in autumn with the snaky plant,
Whose juice is the right madness, the best godship?
Have men, and beasts, and woods, with flower and fruit
From all the earth, one's slaves; bid the worm eat
Your next year's purple from the mulberry leaf,
The tiger shed his skin to line your car,
And men die, thousands in a day, for glory?
Such things should kings bid from their solitude
Upon the top of Man.   Justice and Good,
All penniless, base, earthy kind of fellows,
So low, one wonders they were not born dogs,
Can do as well, alas!

   Adalm.   There's cunning in thee.
A year ago this doctrine might have pleased me:
But since, I have remembered, in my childhood
My teachers told me that I was immortal,
And had within me something like a god;
Now, by believing firmly in that promise,
I do enjoy a part of its fulfilment,
 And, antedating my eternity,

Act as I were immortal.

   Duke.   Think of *now*.
This Hope and Memory are wild horses, tearing
The precious *now* to pieces. Grasp and use
The breath within you; for you know not, whether
That wind about the trees brings you one more.
Thus far yourself. But tell me, hath no other
A right, which you would injure? Is this sceptre,
Which you would stamp to dust and let each varlet
Pick out his grain of power; this great spirit,
This store of mighty men's concentrate souls,
Which kept your fathers in god's breath, and you
Would waste in the wide, smoky, pestilent air
For every dog to snuff in; is this royalty
Your own? O! when you were a boy, young prince,
I would have laid my heart upon your spirit:
Now both are broken.

   Adalm.   Father?

   Duke.   Yes, my son:
We'll live to be most proud of those two names.
Go on thy way: I follow and o'erlook.
This pilgrim's shape will hang about and guard thee,
Being but the shadow of my sunniness,
Looking in patience through a cloudy time.

                          [Exeunt.

SCENE II. *A garden.*

SIBYLLA *and* ATHULF.

Athulf. From me no comfort.   O you specious
        creatures,
So poisonous to the eye!   Go! you sow madness:
And one of you, although I cannot curse her,
Will make my grave a murderer's.   I'll do nought;
But rather drink and revel at your bridal.
And why not Isbrand?   Many such a serpent
Doth lick heaven's dew out of as sweet a flower.
Wed, wed!   I'll not prevent it.
    Sibyl.   I beseech thee,
If there be any tie of love between thee
And her who is thy brother's.
    Athulf.   Curse the word!
And trebly curse the deed that made us brothers!
O that I had been born the man I hate!
Any, at least, but one.   Then—sleep my soul;
And walk not in thy sleep to do the act,
Which thou must ever dream of.   My fair lady,
I would not be the reason of one tear
Upon thy bosom, if the times were other;
If women were not women.   When the world
Turns round the other way, and doing Cain-like

Passes as merrily as doing Eve-like,
Then I'll be pitiful. Let go my hand;
It is a mischievous limb, and may run wild,
Doing the thing its master would not.   [*Exit.*

    Sibyl. Then no one hears me. O! the world's too
       loud,
With trade and battle, for my feeble cry
To rouse the living. The invisible
Hears best what is unspoken; and my thoughts
Have long been calling comfort from the grave.

(WOLFRAM *suddenly appears, in the garment of a*
monk.)

    Wolfr. Lady, you called me.
    Sibyl.   I?
    Wolfr.   The word was *Comfort:*
A name by which the master, whose I am,
Is named by many wise and many wretched.
Will you with me to the place where sighs are not;
A shore of blessing, which disease doth beat
Sea-like, and dashes those whom he would wreck
Into the arms of Peace? But ah! what say I?
You're young and must be merry in the world;
Have friends to envy, lovers to betray you;
And feed young children with the blood of your heart,
Till they have sucked up strength enough to break it.
Poor woman! Art thou nothing but the straw
Bearing a heavy poison, and, that shed,

Cut down to be stamped on ? But thou'rt i' th' blade;
The green and milky sun-deceived grass :
So stand till the scythe comes, take shine and shower,
And the wind fell you gently.

    Sibyl.   Do not go.

Speak as at first you did ; there was in the words
A mystery and music, which did thaw
The hard old rocky world into a flood,
Whereon a swan-drawn boat seemed at my feet
Rocking on its blue billows; and I heard
Harmonies, and breathed odours from an isle,
Whose flowers cast tremulous shadows in the day
Of an immortal sun, and crowd the banks
Whereon immortal human kind doth couch.
This I have dreamt before: your speech recalled it.
So speak to soothe me once again.

    Wolfr. (*aside*)   Snake Death,

Sweet as the cowslip's honey is thy whisper:
O let this dove escape thee ! I'll not plead,
I will not be thy suitor to this innocent:
Open thy craggy jaws; speak, coffin-tongued,
Persuasions through the dancing of the yew-bough
And the crow's nest upon it. (*aloud*) Lady fair,
Listen not to me, look not on me more.
I have a fascination in my words,
A magnet in my look, which drags you downwards,
From hope and life. You set your eyes upon me,
And think I stand upon this earth beside you:

Alas! I am upon a jutting stone,
Which crumbles down the steeps of an abyss;
And you, above me far, grow wild and giddy:
Leave me, or you must fall into the deep.

Sibyl. I leave thee never, nor thou me.   O no!
You know not what a heart you spurn away;
How good it might be, if love cherished it;
And how deserted 'tis; ah! so deserted,
That I have often wished a ghost would come,
Whose love might haunt it.   Turn not thou, the last.
Thou see'st I'm young: how happy might I be!
And yet I only wish these tears I shed
Were raining on my grave.   If thou'lt not love me,
Then do me the next office; show me only
The shortest path to solitary death.

Wolfr. You're moved to wildness, maiden.   Beg
    not of me.
I can grant nothing good: quiet thyself,
And seek heaven's help.   Farewell.

Sibyl.   Wilt thou leave me?
Unpitying, aye unmoved in cheek and heart,
Stern, selfish mortal?   Hast thou heard my prayer;
Hast seen me weep; hast seen my limbs to quiver,
Like a storm-shaken tree over its roots?
Art thou alive, and canst thou see this wretch,
Without a care?

Wolfr.   Thou see'st I am unmoved:
Infer the truth.

I

Sibyl.   Thy soul indeed is dead.

Wolfr. My soul, my soul! O that it wore not now
The semblance of a garb it hath cast off;
O that it was disrobed of these mock limbs,
Shed by a rocky birth unnaturally,
Long after their decease and burial!
O woe that I must speak! for she, who hears,
Is marked for no more breathing. There are histories
Of women, nature's bounties, who disdained
The mortal love of the embodied man,
And sought the solitude which spirits cast
Around their darksome presence. These have loved,
Wooed, wedded, and brought home their moonstruck
          brides
Unto the world-sanded eternity.
Hast faith in such reports?

Sibyl.   So lonely am I,
That I dare wish to prove them true.

Wolfr.   Dar'st die?
A grave-deep question. Answer it religiously.

Sibyl. With him I loved, I dared.

Wolfr.   With me and for me.
I am a ghost. Tremble not; fear not me.
The dead are ever good and innocent,
And love the living. They are cheerful creatures,
And quiet as the sunbeams, and most like,
In grace and patient love and spotless beauty,
The new-born of mankind. 'Tis better too

To die, as thou art, young, in the first grace
And full of beauty, and so be remembered   .
As one chosen from the earth to be an angel;
Not left to droop and wither, and be borne
Down by the breath of time.   Come then, Sibylla,
For I am Wolfram!

  Sibyl.   Thou art come to fetch me!
It is indeed a proof of boundless love,
That thou hadst need of me even in thy bliss.
I go with thee.   O Death! I am thy friend,
I struggle not with thee, I love thy state:
Thou canst be sweet and gentle, be so now;
And let me pass praying away into thee,
As twilight still does into starry night.

        [*The scene closes.*

    Voices in the air.

   As sudden thunder
    Pierces night;
   As magic wonder,
    Wild affright,
   Rives asunder
    Men's delight:
   Our ghost, our corpse; and we
    Rise to be.

   As flies the lizard
    Serpent fell;

As goblin vizard,
At the spell
Of the wizard,
Sinks to hell :
Our life, our laugh, our lay
Pass away.

As wake the morning
Trumpets bright;
As snow-drop, scorning
Winter's might,
Rises warning
Like a spright :
We buried, dead, and slain
Rise again.

SCENE III.

A garden, under the windows of Amala's apartment.

ATHULF.

Athulf. Once more I'll see thee, love, speak to thee,
    hear thee;
And then my soul shall cut itself a door
Out of this planet. I've been wild and heartless,
Laughed at the feasts where Love had never place,
And pledged my light faith to a hundred women,

Forgotten all next day. A worthless life,
A life ridiculous! Day after day,
Folly on folly! But I'll not repent.
Remorse and weeping shall not be my virtues:
Let fools do both, and, having had their evil,
And tickled their young hearts with the sweet sins
That feather Cupid's shafts, turn timid, weep,
Be penitent. Now the wild banquet's o'er,
Wine spilt, lights out, I cannot brook the world,
It is so silent. And that poisonous reptile,
My past self, is a villain I'll not pardon.
I hate and will have vengeance on my soul:
Satirical Murder, help me .. Ha! I am
Devil-inspired: out with you, ye fool's thoughts!
You're young, strong, healthy yet; years may you live:
Why yield to an ill-humoured moment? No!
I'll cut his throat across, make her my wife;
Huzza! for a mad life! and be a Duke!
I was born for sin and love it.

                         O thou villain,
Die, die! Have patience with me, heavenly Mercy!
Let me but once more look upon that blessing,
Then can I calmly offer up to thee
This crime-haired head.

    Enter AMALA *as bride, with a bridesmaid.*
                   O beauty, beauty!
Thou shed'st a moony night of quiet through me.

Thanks! Now I am resolved.

Bridesm.   Amala, good night:
Thou'rt happy. In these high delightful times,
It does the human heart much good to think
On deepest woe, which may be waiting for us,
Masked even in a marriage-hour.

Amala.   Thou'rt timid:
'Tis well to trust in the good genius.
Are not our hearts, in these great pleasures godded,
Let out awhile to their eternity,
And made prophetic? The past is pale to me;
But I do see my future plain of life,
Full of rejoicings and of harvest-dances,
Clearly, it is so sunny. A year hence
I'll laugh at you for this, until you weep.
Good night, sweet fear.

Bridesm.   Take this flower from me,
(A white rose, fitting for a wedding-gift,)
And lay it on your pillow. Pray to live
So fair and innocently; pray to die,
Leaf after leaf, so softly.   [*Exit.*

Amala. —Now to my chamber; yet an hour or two,
In which years must be sown.

Athulf.   Stay Amala;
An old acquaintance brings a greeting to you,
Upon your wedding night.

Amala. His brother Athulf! What can he do here?
I fear the man.

Athulf. Dost love him?

Amala. That were cause
Indeed to fear him. Leave me, leave me, sir:
It is too late. We cannot be together
For any good.

Athulf. This once we can. O Amala,
Had I been in my young days taught the truth,
And brought up with the kindness and affection
Of a good man! I was not myself evil,
But out of youth and ignorance did much wrong.
Had I received lessons in thought and nature,
We might have been together, but not thus.
How then? Did you not love me long ago?
More, O much more than him? Yes, Amala,
You would have been mine now. A life with thee,
Heavenly delight and virtue ever with us!
I've lost it, trod on it, and crush'd it. Woe!
O bitter woe is me!

Amala. Athulf, why make me
Rue the inevitable? Prithee leave me.

Athulf. Thee bye and bye: and all that is not thee.
Thee, my all, that I've forfeited I'll leave,
And the world's all, my nothing.

Amala. Nay; despond not.
Thou'lt be a merry, happy man some day,
And list to this as to a tale of some one
You had forgotten.

Athulf. Now no need of comfort:

I'm somehow glad that it did thus fall out.
Then had I lived too softly; in these woes
I can stand up, and show myself a man.
I do not think that I shall live an hour.
Wilt pardon me for that my earlier deeds
Have caused to thee of sorrow? Amala,
Pity me, pardon me, bless me in this hour;
In this my death, in this your bridal, hour.
Pity me, sweet.

    Amala.   Both thee and me: no more!
    Athulf.   Forgive!
    Amala. With all my soul. God bless thee, my
        dear Athulf.
    Athulf. Kiss I thy hand? O much more fervently
Now, in my grief, than heretofore in love.
Farewell, go; look not back again upon me.
In silence go.   *[Exit Amala.*
          She having left my eyes,
There's nothing in the world, to look on which
I'd live a moment longer. Therefore come,
Thou sacrament of death: Eternity,
I pledge thee thus.   *[He drinks from a vial.*
         How cold and sweet! It seems
As if the earth already began, shaking,
To sink beneath me. O ye dead, come near;
Why see I you not yet? Come, crowd about me;
Under the arch of this triumphal hour,
Welcome me; I am one of you, and one

That, out of love for you, have forced the doors
Of the stale world.

Enter ADALMAR.

Adalm. I'm wearied to the core: where's Amala?
Ha! Near her chambers! Who?
Athulf.   Ask that to-morrow
Of the marble, Adalmar. Come hither to me.
We must be friends: I'm dying.
Adalm.   How?
Athulf.   The cup,
I've drank myself immortal.
Adalm.   You are poisoned?
Athulf. I am blessed, Adalmar. I've done't myself.
'Tis nearly passed, for I begin to hear
Strange but sweet sounds, and the loud rocky dashing
Of waves, where time into Eternity
Falls over ruined worlds. The wind is fair,
The boat is in the bay,
And the fair mermaid pilot calls away.
Adalm. Self poisoned?
Athulf.   Ay: a philosophic deed.
Go and be happy.
Adalm.   God! What hast thou done?
Athulf. Justice upon myself.
Adalm.   No. Thou hast stolen
The right of the deserving good old man
To rest, his cheerful labour being done.

Thou hast been wicked; caused much misery;
Dishonoured maidens; broken fathers' hearts;
Maddened some; made others wicked as thyself;
And darest thou die, leaving a world behind thee
That groans of thee to heaven?

Athulf.   ,   If I thought so—
Terrible would it be: then I've both killed
And damned myself. There's justice!

Adalm.   .   Thou should'st have lived;
Devoting every minute to the work
Of useful, penitent amendment: then,
After long years, you might have knelt to Fate,
And ta'en her blow not fearing. Wretch, thou diest not,
But goest living into hell.

Athulf.   It is too true:
I am deserted by those turbulent joys.
The fiend had made me death-drunk. Here I'll lie,
And die most wretchedly, accursed, unpitied
Of all, most hated by myself. O God,
If thou could'st but repeal this fatal hour,
And let me live, how day and night I'd toil
For all things to atone! Must I wish vainly?
My brother, is there any way to live?

Adalm. For thee, alas! in this world there is none.
Think not upon't.

Athulf.   Thou liest: there must be:
Thou know'st it, and dost keep it secret from me,
Letting me die for hate and jealousy.

O that I had not been so pious a fool,
But killed thee, 'stead of me, and had thy wife!
I should be at the banquet, drinking to her,
Kissing her lip, in her eye smiling. . .

                          Peace!

Thou see'st I'm growing mad: now leave me here,
Accursed as I am, alone to die.

    Adalm. . Wretched, yet not despised, farewell my
      brother.

    Athulf. O Arab, Arab! Thou dost sell true drugs.
Brother, my soul is very weary now:
Speak comfortably to me.

    Adalm.   From the Arab,
From Ziba, had'st the poison?

    Athulf.   Ay. 'Twas good:
An honest villain is he.

    Adalm.   Hold, sweet brother,
A little longer hold in hope on life;
But a few minutes more. I seek the sorcerer,
And he shall cure thee with some wondrous drug.
He can, and shall perform it: rest thee quiet:
Hope or revenge I'll bring thee.   [*Exit.*

    Athulf.   Dare I hope?
O no: methinks it is not so unlovely,
This calm unconscious state, this breathless peace,
Which all, but troublesome and riotous man,
Assume without resistance. Here I'll lay me,
And let life fall from off me tranquilly.

[*Enter singers and musicians led by* SIEGFRIED;
*they play under the windows of Amala's apart-
ment, and sing.*]

Song.

By female voices.

We have bathed, where none have seen us,
 In the lake and in the fountain,
  Underneath the charmed statue
Of the timid, bending Venus,
 When the water-nymphs were counting
In the waves the stars of night,
  And those maidens started at you,
Your limbs shone through so soft and bright.
  But no secrets dare we tell,
   For thy slaves unlace thee,
   And he, who shall embrace thee,
  Waits to try thy beauty's spell.

By male voices.

We have crowned thee queen of women,
 Since love's love, the rose, hath kept her
  Court within thy lips and blushes,
And thine eye, in beauty swimming,
 Kissing, we rendered up the sceptre,
At whose touch the startled soul
  Like an ocean bounds and gushes,

And spirits bend at thy controul.
   But no secrets dare we tell,
     For thy slaves unlace thee,
     And he, who shall embrace thee,
   Is at hand, and so farewell.

Athulf. Shame on you! Do you sing their bridal
   song
Ere I have closed mine eyes? Who's there among you
That dare to be enamoured of a maid
So far above you, ye poor rhyming knaves?
Ha! there begins another.

Song by Siegfried.

Lady, was it fair of thee
To seem so passing fair to me?
  Not every star to every eye
   Is fair; and why
Art thou another's share?
  Did thine eyes shed brighter glances,
Thine unkissed bosom heave more fair,
  To his than to my fancies?
   But I'll forgive thee still;
   Thou'rt fair without thy will.
   So be: but never know,
   That 'tis the hue of woe.

Lady, was it fair of thee

To be so gentle still to me?
Not every lip to every eye
Should let smiles fly.
Why didst thou never frown,
To frighten from my pillow
Love's head, round which Hope wove a crown,
And saw not 'twas of willow?
But I'll forgive thee still;
Thou knew'st not smiles could kill.
Smile on : but never know,
I die, nor of what woe.

Athulf. Ha! Ha! That fellow moves my spleen;
A disappointed and contented lover.
Methinks he's above fifty by his voice:
If not, he should be whipped about the town,
For vending such tame doctrine in love-verses.
Up to the window, carry off the bride,
And away on horseback, squeaker!
    Siegfr. Peace, thou bold drunken fellow that liest
      there!—
Leave him to sleep his folly out, good fellows.
              [*Exit with musicians.*
    Athulf. Well said: I do deserve it. I lie here
A thousand-fold fool, dying ridiculously
Because I could not have the girl I fancied.
Well, they are wedded; how long now will last
Affection or content? Besides 'twere possible

He might have quaffed a like draught. But 'tis done :
Villanous idiot that I am to think on't.
She willed it so. Then Amala, be fearless :
Wait but a little longer in thy chamber,
And he will be with thee whom thou hast chosen :
Or, if it make thee pastime, listen sweet one,
And I will sing to thee, here in the moonlight,
Thy bridal song and my own dirge in one.

He sings.

A cypress-bough, and a rose-wreath sweet,
A wedding-robe, and a winding-sheet,
     A bridal-bed and a bier.
Thine be the kisses, maid,
     And smiling Love's alarms ;
And thou, pale youth, be laid
     In the grave's cold arms.
Each in his own charms,
     Death and Hymen both are here ;
          So up with scythe and torch,
          And to the old church porch,
     While all the bells ring clear :
And rosy, rosy the bed shall bloom,
And earthy, earthy heap up the tomb.

Now tremble dimples on your cheek,
Sweet be your lips to taste and speak,
     For he who kisses is near :

By her the bridegod fair,
  In youthful power and force ;
By him the grizard bare,
  Pale knight on a pale horse,
  To woo him to a corpse.

  Death and Hymen both are here ;
    So up with scythe and torch,
    And to the old church porch,
  While all the bells ring clear :
  And rosy, rosy the bed shall bloom,
  And earthy, earthy heap up the tomb.

Athulf. Now we'll lie down and wait for our two
    summoners ;
Each patiently at least.

Enter AMALA.

            O thou kind girl,
Art thou again there ? Come and lay thine hand
In mine ; and speak again thy soft way to me.
  Amala. Thy voice is fainter, Athulf : why sang'st
    thou ?
  Athulf. It was my farewell : now I'll sing no more ;
Nor speak a great deal after this. 'Tis well
You weep not. If you had esteemed me much,
It were a horrible mistake of mine.
Wilt close my eyes when I am dead, sweet maid ?
  Amala. O Athulf, thou might'st still have lived.

Athulf.   What boots it,
And thou not mine, nor even loving me?
But that makes dying very sad to me.
Yet even thy pity is worth much.

Amala.   O no;
I pity not alone, but I am wretched,—
Love thee and ever did most fervently,
Still hoping thou would'st turn and merit it.
But now—O God! if life were possible to thee,
I'd be thy friend for ever.

Athulf. O thou art full of blessings!
Thou lovest me, Amala: one kiss, but one;
It is not much to grant a dying man.

Amala. I am thy brother's bride, forget not that;
And never but to this, thy dying ear,
Had I confessed so much in such an hour.
But this be too forgiven.   Now farewell.
'Twere not amiss if I should die to-night:
Athulf, my love, my only love, farewell.

Athulf. Yet one more minute. If we meet hereafter,
Wilt thou be mine? I have the right to thee;
And, if thou promise, I will let him live
This life, unenvied, with thee.

Amala.   I will, Athulf:
Our bliss there will be greater for the sorrow
We now in parting feel.

Athulf.   I go, to wait thee. [*Exit Amala.*
Farewell, my bliss! She loves me with her soul,

K

And I might have enjoyed her, were he fallen.
Ha! ha! and I am dying like a rat,
And he shall drink his wine, twenty years hence,
Beside his cherished wife, and speak of me
With a compassionate smile! Come, Madness, come,
For death is loitering still.

Enter ADALMAR *and* ZIBA.

Adalm.   An antidote!
Restore him whom thy poisons have laid low,
If thou wilt not sup with thy fellow fiends
In hell to-night.
      Ziba.   I pray thee strike me not.
It was his choice; and why should he be breathing
Against his will?
      Athulf.   Ziba, I need not perish.
Now my intents are changed: so, if thou canst,
Dispense me life again.
      Adalm.   Listen to him, slave,
And once be a preserver.
      Ziba.   Let him rise.
Why, think you that I'd deal a benefit,
So precious to the noble as is death,
To such a pampered darling of delight
As he that shivers there? O, not for him,
Blooms my dark Nightshade, nor doth Hemlock brew
Murder for cups within her cavernous root.
Not for him is the metal blessed to kill,

Nor lets the poppy her leaves fall for him.
To heroes such are sacred. He may live,
As long as 'tis the Gout and Dropsy's pleasure.
He wished to play at suicide, and swallowed
A draught, that may depress and shake his powers
Until he sleeps awhile; then all is o'er.
And so good night, my princes.   [*Exit.*

   Adalm.   Dost thou hear?

   Athulf. Victory! victory! I *do* hear; and Fate
     hears,
And plays with Life for one of our two souls,
With dice made of death's bones. But shall I do't?
O Heaven! it is a fearful thing to be so saved!

   Adalm. Now, brother, thou'lt be happy.

   Athulf.   With thy wife!
I tell thee, hapless brother, on my soul,
Now that I live, I *will* live; I alone;
And Amala alone shall be my love.
There's no more room for you, since you have chosen
The woman and the power which I covet.
Out of thy bridal bed, out of thy throne!
Away to Abel's grave.   [*Stabs Adalmar.*

   Adalm.   Thou murderous fiend!
I was thy brother.   [*dies.*

   Athulf. (*after a pause*) How long a time it is since
     I was here!
And yet I know not whether I have slept,
Or wandered through a dreary cavernous forest,

Struggling with monsters. 'Tis a quiet place,
And one inviting strangely to deep rest.
I have forgotten something; my whole life
Seems to have vanished from me to this hour.
There was a foe whom I should guard against;
Who is he?

    Amala. (*from her window*) Adalmar!

    Athulf. (*in a low voice*) Hush! hush! I come to
      thee.

Let me but see if he be dead: speak gently,
His jealous ghost still hears.

    Amala.   So, it is over

With that poor troubled heart! O then to-night
Leave me alone to weep.

    Athulf.   As thou wilt, lady.

I'm stunned with what has happened. He is dead.

    Amala. O night of sorrow! Bear him from the
      threshold.

None of my servants must know where and why
He sought his grave. Remove him. O poor Athulf,
Why did'st thou it? I'll to my bed and mourn.

                        [*retires.*

    Athulf. Hear'st thou, corpse, how I play thy part?
      Thus had he

Pitied me in fraternal charity,
And I lain there so helpless. Precious cup,
A few drops more of thy somniferous balm,
To keep out spectres from my dreams to-night:
My eyelids thirst for slumber. But what's this,

That chills my blood and darkens so my eyes?
What's going on in my heart and in my brain,
My bones, my life, all over me, all through me?
It cannot last. No longer shall I be
What I am now. O I am changing, changing,
Dreadfully changing! Even here and now
A transformation will o'ertake me.   Hark!
It is God's sentence muttered over me.
I am unsouled, dishumanized, uncreated;
My passions swell and grow like brutes conceived;
My feet are fixing roots, and every limb
Is billowy and gigantic, till I seem
A wild, old, wicked mountain in the air:
And the abhorred conscience of this murder,
It will grow up a lion, all alone,
A mighty-maned, grave-mouthed prodigy,
And lair him in my caves: and other thoughts,
Some will be snakes, and bears, and savage wolves:
And when I lie tremendous in the desart,
Or abandoned sea, murderers and idiot men
Will come to live upon my rugged sides,
Die, and be buried in me.   Now it comes;
I break, and magnify, and lose my form.
And yet I shall be taken for a man,
And never be discovered till I die.
Terrible, terrible: damned before my time,
In secret! 'Tis a dread, o'erpowering phantom.
            (*He lies down by the body, and sleeps: the*
                    scene closes.)

SCENE IV.

A large hall in the ducal castle. Through the windows in the back ground appears the illuminated city.

Enter ISBRAND *and* SIEGFRIED.

Isbr. By my grave, Siegfried, 'tis a wedding-night.
The wish, that I have courted from my boyhood,
Comes blooming, crowned, to my embrace. Methinks,
The spirit of the city is right lovely;
And she will leave her rocky body sleeping,
To-night, to be my queenly paramour.
Has it gone twelve?

Siegfr.   This half hour.   Here I've set
A little clock, that you may mark the time.

Isbr. Its hand divides the hour.   Are our guards
        here,
About the castle?

Siegfr.   You've a thousand swordsmen,
Strong and true soldiers, at the stroke of one.

Isbr. One's a good hour; a ghostly hour. To-night
The ghost of a dead planet shall walk through,
And shake the pillars of this dukedom down.
The princes both are occupied and lodged
Far from us: that is well; they will hear little.

Go once more round, to the towers and battlements:
The bell, that strikes, says to our hearts ' Be one ;'
And, with one motion of a hundred arms,
Be the beacons fixed, the alarums rung,
And tyrants slain ! Be busy.

  Siegfr.   I am with them.
               [Exit.

Isbr. Mine is the hour it strikes ; my first of life.
To-morrow, with what pity and contempt,
Shall I look back new-born upon myself !

      Enter a servant.

            What now ?
  Servant. The banquet's ready.
  Isbr.   Let it wait awhile :
The wedding is not ended. That shall be
No common banquet : none sit there, but souls
That have outlived a lower state of being.
Summon the guests.   *[Exit servant.*
     Some shall have bitter cups,
The honest shall be banished from the board,
And the knaves duped by a luxurious bait.

 Enter the DUKE, THORWALD, *and other guests.*

Friends, welcome hither in the prince's name,
Who has appointed me his deputy
To-night. Why this is right : while men are here,
They should keep close and warm and thick together;

Many abreast. Our middle life is broad ;
But birth and death, the turnstiles that admit us
On earth and off it, send us, one by one,
A solitary walk. Lord governor,
Will you not sit? ↓

Thorw.   You are a thrifty liver,
Keeping the measure of your time beside you.

Isbr. Sir, I'm a melancholy, lonely man,
A kind of hermit : and to meditate
Is all my being. One has said, that time
Is a great river running to eternity.
Methinks 'tis all one water, and the fragments,
That crumble off our ever-dwindling life,
Dropping into't, first make the twelve-houred circle,
And that spreads outwards to the great round Ever.

Thorw. You're fanciful.

Isbr.   A very ballad-maker.
We quiet men must think and dream at least.
Who likes a rhyme among us? My lord governor,
'Tis tedious waiting until supper time :
Shall I read some of my new poetry ?
One piece at least?

Thorw.   Well ; without further preface,
If it be brief.

Isbr.   A fragment, quite unfinished,
Of a new ballad called ' The Median Supper.'
It is about Astyages; and I
Differ in somewhat from Herodotus.

But altering the facts of history,
When they are troublesome, good governors
Will hardly visit rigorously.   Attention!

    (*reads*) " Harpagus, hast thou salt enough,
     " Hast thou broth enough to thy kid?
    " And hath the cook put right good stuff
     " Under the pasty lid?"

    " I've salt enough, Astyages,
     " And broth enough in sooth;
    " And the cook hath mixed the meat and grease
     " Most tickling to my tooth."

So spake no wild red Indian swine,
    Eating a forest rattle-snake:
But Harpagus, that Mede of mine,
    And king Astyages so spake.

    " Wilt have some fruit?   Wilt have some wine?
     "Here's what is soft to chew;
    " I plucked it from a tree divine,
     " More precious never grew."

Harpagus took the basket up,
    Harpagus brushed the leaves away;
But first he filled a brimming cup,
    For his heart was light and gay.

And then he looked, and saw a face,
  Chopped from the shoulders of some one;
And who alone could smile in grace
  So sweet? Why, Harpagus, thy son.

" Alas!" quoth the king, " I've no fork,
  " Alas! I've no spoon of relief,
" Alas! I've no neck of a stork
  " To push down this throttling grief.

" We've played at kid for child, lost both;
  " I'd give you the limbs if I could;
" Some lie in your platter of broth:
  " Good night, and digestion be good."

Now Harpagus said not a word,
  Did no eye-water spill:
His heart replied, for that had heard;
  And hearts' replies are still.

How do you like it?
  Duke.   Poetry, they say,
Should be the poet's soul; and here, methinks,
In every word speaks yours.
  Isbr.   Good. Do'nt be glad too soon.
Do ye think I've done? Three minutes' patience more.

A cannibal of his own boy,
  He is a cannibal uncommon;

And Harpagus, he is my joy,
　Because he wept not like a woman.

From the old supper-giver's pole
　He tore the many-kingdomed mitre;
To him, who cost him his son's soul,
　He gave it; to the Persian fighter:
　　　　　　And quoth,
" Old art thou, but a fool in blood:
" If thou hast made me eat my son,
" Cyrus hath ta'en his grandsire's food;
" There's kid for child, and who has won?

" All kingdomless is thy old head,
" In which began the tyrannous fun;
" Thou'rt slave to him, who should be dead:
" There's kid for child, and who has won?"

Now let the clock strike, let the clock strike now,
And world be altered!
　　　(*The clock strikes one, and the hour is repeated
　　　　from the steeples of the city.*)
　　　　　　　Trusty time-piece,
Thou hast struck a mighty hour, and thy work's done;
For never shalt thou count a meaner one.
　　　　　　　[*He dashes it on the ground.*
Thus let us break our old life of dull hours,
And hence begin a being, counted not

By minutes, but by glories and delights.

> (*He steps to a window and throws it open.*

Thou steepled city, that dost lie below,
Time doth demand whether thou wilt be free.
Now give thine answer.

> (*A trumpet is heard, followed by a peal of
> cannon. Beacons are fixed, &c. The stage
> is lined with soldiery.*)

   Thorw.   Traitor, desperate traitor!
Yet betrayed traitor! Make a path for me,
Or, by the majesty that thou offendest,
Thou shalt be struck with lightning in thy triumph.

> *Isbr. All kingdomless is the old mule,*
>   *In whom began the tyrannous fun;*
> *Thou'rt slave to him, who was thy fool;*
>   *There's Duke for Brother; who has won?*

Take the old man away.
   Thorw.   I go: but my revenge
Hangs, in its unseen might, godlike around you.

> [*Exit guarded.*

   Isbr. To work, my friends, to work! Each man
     his way.
These present instants, cling to them; hold fast;
And spring from this one to the next, still upwards.
They're rungs of Jacob's heaven-scaling ladder:
Haste, or 'tis drawn away.   [*Exeunt cæteri.*

                    O stingy nature,
To make me but one man! Had I but body
For every several measure of thought and will,
This night should see me world-crowned.

                    Enter a messenger.

                        What news bring'st thou?
Messr. Friends of the governor hold the strongest
    tower,
And shoot with death's own arrows.
Isbr.   Get thee back,
And never let me hear thy voice again,
Unless to say, " 'tis taken."   Hark ye, sirrah;
Wood in its walls, lead on its roof, the tower
Cries, "Burn me!" Go and cut away the draw-bridge,
And leave the quiet fire to himself:
He knows his business.   [*Exit messenger.*

                Enter ZIBA *armed.*

                    What with you?
Ziba.   I'll answer,
When one of us is undermost.
Isbr.   Ha! Midnight,
Can a slave fight?
Ziba.   None better.   Come; we'll struggle,
And roar, and dash, and tumble in our rage,
As doth the long-jawed, piteous crocodile
With the blood-howling hippopotamus,

In quaking Nile.

 Isbr.   Not quite so great; but rather,
Like to a Hercules of crockery
Slaying a Nemean lion of barley-sugar,
On a twelfth cake. [*They fight: Ziba is disarmed.*
     Now darest thou cry for mercy?

 Ziba. Never. Eternity! Come give me that,
And I will thank thee.

 Isbr.   Something like a man,
And something like a fool. Thou'rt such a reptile,
That I do like thee: pick up thy black life:
I would not make my brother King and Fool,
Friend Death, so poor a present. Hence!
         [*Exit Ziba.*
       They're busy.
'Tis a hot hour, which Murder steals from Love,
To beget ghosts in.

    Enter SIEGFRIED.

     Now?

 Siegfr. Triumph! They cannot stand another half
  hour.
The loyal had all supped and gone to bed:
When our alarums thundered, they could only
Gaze from their frighted windows: and some few
We had in towers and churches to besiege.
But, when one hornet's nest was burnt, the rest
Cried quarter, and went home to end their naps.

Isbr. 'Twas good. I knew it was well planned.
Return,
And finish all. I'll follow thee, and see
How Mars looks in his night-cap. [*Exit Siegfried.*
O! it is nothing now to be a man.
Adam, thy soul was happy that it wore
The first, new, mortal members. To have felt
The joy of the first year, when the one spirit
Kept house-warming within its fresh-built clay,
I'd be content to be as old a ghost.
Thine was the hour to live in. Now we're common,
And man is tired of being merely human ;
And I'll be something more : yet, not by tearing
This chrysalis of psyche ere its hour,
Will I break through Elysium. There are sometimes,
Even here, the means of being more than men :
And I by wine, and women, and the sceptre,
Will be, my own way, heavenly in my clay.
O you small star-mob, had I been one of you,
I would have seized the sky some moonless night,
And made myself the sun ; whose morrow rising
Shall see me new-created by myself.
Come, come ; to rest, my soul. I must sleep off
This old plebeian creature that I am.   [*Exit.*

ACT V.

SCENE I.

An apartment in the ducal castle.

ISBRAND *and* SIEGFRIED.

Siegfr. THEY still wait for you in their council
    chamber,
And clamorously demand the keys of the treasure,
The stores of arms, lists of the troops you've hired,
Reports of your past acts, and your intentions
Towards the new republic.
    Isbr.   They demand!
A phrase politer would have pleased me better.
The puppets, whose heart strings I hold and play
Between my thumb and fingers, this way, that way;
Through whose masks, wrinkled o'er by age and passion,
My voice and spirit hath spoken continually;
Dare now to ape free will? Well done, Prometheus!
Thou'st pitied Punch and given him a soul,
And all his wooden peers. The tools I've used
To chisel an old heap of stony laws,
The abandoned sepulchre of a dead dukedom,
Into the form my spirit loved and longed for;

Now that I've perfected her beauteous shape,
And animated it with half my ghost;
Now that I lead her to our bridal bed,
Dare the mean instruments to lay their plea,
Or their demand forsooth, between us? Go;
And tell the fools, (you'll find them pale, and dropping
Cold tears of fear out of their trembling cheek-pores;)
Tell them, for comfort, that I only laughed;
And bid them all to sup with me to-night,
When we will call the cup to counsel.

Siegfr.   Mean you
Openly to assume a kingly power,
Nor rather inch yourself into the throne?
Perhaps—but as you will.

Isbr.   Siegfried, I'm one
That what I will must do, and what I do
Do in the nick of time without delay.
To-morrow is the greatest fool I know,
Excepting those who put their trust in him.
In one word hear, what soon they all shall hear:
A king's a man, and I will be no man
Unless I am a king. Why, where's the difference?
Throne-steps divide us: they're soon climbed perhaps:
I have a bit of FIAT in my soul,
And can myself create my little world.
Had I been born a four-legged child, methinks
I might have found the steps from dog to man,
And crept into his nature. Are there not

L

Those that fall down out of humanity,
Into the story where the four-legged dwell?
But to the conclave with my message quickly:
I've got a deal to do.   [*Exit Siegfried.*
                              How I despise
All such mere men of muscle! It was ever
My study to find out a way to godhead,
And on reflection soon I found that first
I was but half created; that a power
Was wanting in my soul to be its soul,
And this was mine to make.   Therefore I fashioned
A will above my will, that plays upon it,
As the first soul doth use in men and cattle.
There's lifeless matter; add the power of shaping,
And you've the crystal: add again the organs,
Wherewith to subdue sustenance to the form
And manner of one's self, and you've the plant:
Add power of motion, senses, and so forth,
And you've all kinds of beasts; suppose a pig:
To pig add reason, foresight, and such stuff,
Then you have man.   What shall we add to man,
To bring him higher? I begin to think
That's a discovery I soon shall make.
Thus, owing nought to books, but being read
In the odd nature of much fish and fowl,
And cabbages and beasts, I've raised myself,
By this comparative philosophy,
Above your shoulders, my sage gentlemen.

Have patience but a little, and keep still,
I'll find means, bye and bye, of flying higher.

[*Exit.*

SCENE II.

Another apartment.

The DUKE, SIEGFRIED, MARIO, ZIBA *and*
conspirators.

A conspirator (to Siegfried) Said he nought else ?
Siegfr.   What else he said was worse.
He is no more Isbrand of yesterday ;
But looks and talks like one, who in the night
Hath made a bloody compact with some fiend.
His being is grown greater than it was,
And must make room, by cutting off men's lives,
For its shadowy increase.
Conspir.   O friends, what have we done ?
Sold, for a promise, still security,
The mild familiar laws our fathers left us ;
Uprooted our firm country.
Ziba.   And now sit,
Weeping like babes, among its ruins. Up !
You have been cheated ; now turn round upon him.
In this his triumph pull away his throne,
And let him into hell.
Another conspir.   But that I heard it

From you, his inmost counsel and next heart,
I'd not believe it. Why, the man was open ;
We looked on him, and saw our looks reflected ;
Our hopes and wishes found an echo in him ;
He pleased us all, I think. Let's doubt the worst,
Until we see.

    Duke.   Until you feel and perish.

You looked on him, and saw your looks reflected,
Because his soul was in a dark deep well,
And must draw down all others to increase it :
Your hopes and wishes found an echo in him,
As out of a sepulchral cave, prepared
For you and them to sleep in. To be brief,
He is the foe of all ; let all be his,
And he must be o'erwhelmed.

    Siegfr.   I throw him off,
Although I feared to say so in his presence,
And think you all will fear. O that we had
Our good old noble Duke, to help us here !

    Duke. Of him I have intelligence. The governor,
Whose guards are bribed and awed by these good tidings,
Waits us within. There we will speak at large :
And O ! may justice, for this once, descend
Like lightning-footed vengeance.

    Mario.   It will come ;
But when, I know not. Liberty, whose shade
Attends, smiles still in patience, and that smile
Melts tyrants down in time : and, till she bids,

To strike were unavailing.

                     [Exeunt all but Siegfried and Ziba.

    Ziba.   Let them talk:

I mean to do; and will let no one's thoughts,

Or reasonable cooling counsels, mix

In my resolve to weaken it, as little

As shall a drop of rain or pity-water

Adulterate this thick blood-curdling liquor.

Siegfried, I'll free you from this thankless master.

    Siegfr. I understand. To-night? Why that is best.

Man's greatest secret, like the earth's, the devil,

Slips through a key-hole or the smallest chink.

In plottings there is still some crack unstopped,

Some heart not air-tight, some fellow who doth talk

In sleep or in his cups, or tells his tale,

Love-drunk, unto his secret-selling mistress.

How shall't be done though?

    Ziba.   I'm his cup-bearer;

An office that he gave me in derision,

And I will execute so cunningly

That he shall have no lips, to laugh with, long;

Nor spare and spurn me, as he did last night.

Let him beware, who shows a dogged slave

Pity or mercy! For the drug, 'tis good:

There is a little, hairy, green-eyed snake,

Of voice like to the woody nightingale,

And ever singing pitifully sweet,

That nestles in the barry bones of death,

And is his dearest pet and play-fellow.
The honied froth about that serpent's tongue
Deserves not so his habitation's name,
As doth the cup that I shall serve to him.

                  [*Exeunt.*

SCENE III.

A meadow.

SIBYLLA *and ladies, gathering flowers.*

Sibyl. Enough; the dew falls, and the glow-worm's
    shining:
Now let us search our baskets for the fairest
Among our flowery booty, and then sort them.
    Lady. The snow-drops are all gone; but here are
    cowslips,
And primroses, upon whose petals maidens,
Who love to find a moral in all things,
May read a lesson of pale bashfulness;
And violets, that have taught their young buds whiteness,
That blue-eyed ladies' lovers might not tear them
For the old comparison; daisies without number,
And butter-cups and lilies of the vale.
    Sibyl. Sit then; and we will bind some up with rushes,
And wind us garlands. Thus it is with man;
He looks on nature as his supplement,

And still will find out likenesses and tokens
Of consanguinity, in the world's graces,
To his own being.   So he loves the rose,
For the cheek's sake, whose touch is the most grateful
At night-fall to his lip ; and, as the stars rise,
Welcomes the memories of delighting glances,
Which go up as an answer o'er his soul.

   Lady. And therefore earth and all its ornaments,
Which are the symbols of humanity
In forms refined, and efforts uncompleted,
Graceful and innocent, temper the heart,
Of him who muses and compares them skilfully,
To glad belief and tearful gratitude.
This is the sacred source of poesy.

   Sibyl. While we are young, and free from care, we
      think so.
But, when old age or sorrow brings us nearer
To spirits and their interests, we see
Few features of mankind in outward nature ;
But rather signs inviting us to heaven.
I love flowers too ; not for a young girl's reason,
But because these brief visitors to us
Rise yearly from the neighbourhood of the dead,
To show us how far fairer and more lovely
Their world is ; and return thither again,
Like parting friends that beckon us to follow,
And lead the way silent and smilingly.
Fair is the season when they come to us,

Unfolding the delights of that existence
Which is below us : 'tis the time of spirits,
Who with the flowers, and like them, leave their graves:
But when the earth is sealed, and none dare come
Upwards to cheer us, and man's left alone,
We have cold, cutting winter.   For no bridal,
Excepting with the grave, are flowers fit emblems.

    Lady.   And why then do we pluck and wreathe them
        now ?

    Sibyl.   Because a bridal with the grave is near.
You will have need of them to strew a corpse.
Ay, maidens, I am dying ; but lament not :
It is to me a wished for change of being.
Yonder behold the evening star arising,
Appearing bright over the mountain-tops ;
He has just died out of another region,
Perhaps a cloudy one ; and so die I ;
And the high heaven, serene and light with joy,
Which I pass into, will be my love's soul,
That will encompass me ; and I shall tremble,
A brilliant star of never-dying delight,
Mid the ethereal depth of his eternity.
Now lead me homewards : and I'll lay me down,
To sleep not, but to rest : then strew me o'er
With these flowers fresh out of the ghosts' abodes,
And they will lead me softly down to them.
                              [*Exeunt.*

SCENE IV.

*The ruined cathedral, the sepulchre, and the clois-
ters; on which latter is painted the* DANCE OF
DEATH. *In the foreground a large covered
table, with empty chairs set round it. Moonlight.
The clock strikes twelve; on which is heard a*

Song in the air.

The moon doth mock and make me crazy,
   And midnight tolls her horrid claim
   On ghostly homage.   Fie, for shame!
Deaths, to stand painted there so lazy.
There's nothing but the stars about us,
   And they're no tell-tales, but shine quiet:
   Come out, and hold a midnight riot,
Where no mortal fool dare flout us:
And, as we rattle in the moonlight pale ;
Wanderers shall think 'tis the nightingale.

*(The Deaths, and the figures paired with them,
come out of the walls: some seat themselves at
the table, and appear to feast, with mocking
gestures; others dance fantastically to a
rattling music, singing)*

Mummies and skeletons, out of your stones ;
   Every age, every fashion, and figure of Death :

The death of the giant with petrified bones ;
    The death of the infant who never drew breath.
Little and gristly, or bony and big,
    White and clattering, grassy and yellow ;
The partners are waiting, so strike up a jig,
    Dance and be merry, for Death's a droll fellow.
The emperor and empress, the king and the queen,
    The knight and the abbot, friar fat, friar thin,
The gipsy and beggar, are met on the green ;
    Where's Death and his sweetheart ? We want to
      begin.
In circles, and mazes, and many a figure,
    Through clouds, over chimnies and corn-fields yellow,
We'll dance and laugh at the red-nosed grave-digger,
    Who dreams not that Death is so merry a fellow.

        (One with a scythe, who has stood sentinel,
                now sings)

    Although my old ear
      Hath neither hammer nor drum,
    Methinks I can hear
      Living skeletons come.
    The cloister re-echoes the call,
      And it frightens the lizard,
    And, like an old hen, the wall
      Cries " cluck ! cluck ! back to my gizzard ;
      " 'Tis warm, though it's stony,
      " My chickens so bony."

So come let us hide, each with his bride,
For the wicked are coming who have not yet died.

*(The figures return to their places
in the wall.)*

Enter ISBRAND, *the* DUKE, SIEGFRIED, MARIO,
WOLFRAM *as fool, and conspirators, followed by*
ZIBA *and other attendants.*

Isbr. You wonder at my banqueting-house perhaps :
But 'tis my fashion, when the sky is clear,
To drink my wine out in the open air :
And this our sometime meeting-place is shadowy,
And the wind howleth through the ruins bravely.
Now sit, my gentle guests : and you, dark man,

[*to Wolfr.*

Make us as merry as you can, and proudly
Bear the new office, which your friend, the pilgrim,
Has begged for you : 'twas my profession once ;
Do justice to that cap.

*(They sit round the table, and partake of the
feast, making gestures somewhat similar to
those mocked by the figures.)*

Duke. Now, having washed our hearts of love and
   sorrow,
And pledged the rosiness of many a cheek,
And, with the name of many a lustrous maiden,
Ennobled enough cups ; feed, once again,
Our hearing with another merry song.

Isbr. 'Tis pity that the music of this dukedom,
Under the former government, went wrong,
Like all the rest: my ministers shall look to't.
But sing again, my men.

    Siegfr.   What shall it be,
And of what turn? Shall battle's drum be heard?
The chase's trumpet? Shall the noise of Bacchus
Swell in our cheeks, or lazy, sorrowing love
Burthen with sighs our ballad?

    Isbr.   Try the piece,
You sang me yesternight to sleep with best.
It is for such most profitable ends
We crowned folks encourage all the arts.

Song.

My goblet's golden lips are dry,
  And, as the rose doth pine
  For dew, so doth for wine
    My goblet's cup;
Rain, O! rain, or it will die;
    Rain, fill it up!

Arise, and get thee wings to-night,
  Ætna! and let run o'er
  Thy wines, a hill no more,
    But darkly frown
A cloud, where eagles dare not soar,
    Dropping rain down.

Isbr. A very good and thirsty melody :
What say you to it, my court poet ?

Wolfr. Good melody ! If this be a good melody,
I have at home, fattening in my stye,
A sow that grunts above the nightingale.
Why this will serve for those, who feed their veins
With crust, and cheese of dandelion's milk,
And the pure Rhine.   When I am sick o' mornings,
With a horn-spoon tinkling my porridge-pot,
'Tis a brave ballad : but in Bacchanal night,
O'er wine, red, black, or purple-bubbling wine,
That takes a man by the brain and whirls him round,
By Bacchus' lip ! I like a full-voiced fellow,
A craggy-throated, fat-cheeked trumpeter,
A barker, a moon-howler, who could sing
Thus, as I heard the snaky mermaids sing
In Phlegethon, that hydrophobic river,
One May-morning in Hell.

Song.

Old Adam, the carrion crow,
  The old crow of Cairo ;
He sat in the shower, and let it flow
  Under his tail and over his crest ;
    And through every feather
    Leaked the wet weather ;
  And the bough swung under his nest ;
For his beak it was heavy with marrow.

Is that the wind dying? O no;
It's only two devils, that blow
Through a murderer's bones, to and fro,
In the ghosts' moonshine.

Ho! Eve, my grey carrion wife,
    When we have supped on kings' marrow,
Where shall we drink and make merry our life?
    Our nest it is queen Cleopatra's skull,
        'Tis cloven and cracked,
        And battered and hacked,
    But with tears of blue eyes it is full:
    Let us drink then, my raven of Cairo.
    Is that the wind dying? O no;
    It's only two devils, that blow
    Through a murderer's bones, to and fro,
        In the ghosts' moonshine.

Isbr. Pilgrim, it is with pleasure I acknowledge,
In this your friend, a man of genuine taste:
He imitates my style in prose and verse:
And be assured that this deserving man
Shall soon be knighted, when I have invented
The name of my new order; and perhaps
I'll make him minister. I pledge you, Fool:
Black! something exquisite.
    Ziba.   Here's wine of Egypt,
Found in a Memphian cellar, and perchance .

Pressed from its fruit to wash Sesostris' throat,
Or sweeten the hot palate of Cambyses.
See how it pours, thick, clear, and odorous.

    Isbr. 'Tis full, without a bubble on the top:
Pour him the like. Now give a toast.

    Wolfr.   Excuse me:
I might offend perhaps, being blunt, a stranger,
And rustically speaking rustic thoughts.

    Isbr. That shall not be: give us what toast you will,
We'll empty all our goblets at the word,
Without demur.

    Siegfr.   Well, since the stranger's silent,
I'll give a toast, which, I can warrant you,
Was yet ne'er drunk. There is a bony man,
Through whom the sun shines, when the sun is out;
Or the rain drops, when any clouds are weeping;
Or the wind blows, if Œolus will; his name,
And let us drink to his success and sanity;—
But will you truly?

    Isbr.   Truly, as I said.

    Siegfr. Then round with the health of Death, round
        with the health
Of Death the bony, Death the great; round, round.
Empty yourselves, all cups, unto the health
Of great King Death!

    Wolfr. Set down the cup, Isbrand, set the cup down.
Drink not, I say.

    Siegfr.   And what's the matter now?

Isbr. What do you mean, by bidding me not drink?
Answer, I'm thirsty.

Wolfr.   Push aside the boughs:
Let's see the night, and let the night see us.

 Isbr. Will the fool read us astronomic lectures?

 Wolfr. Above stars; stars below; round the moon
  stars.
Isbrand, don't sip the grape-juice.

 Isbr.   Must I drink,
Or not, according to a horoscope?
Says Jupiter, no? Then he's a hypocrite.

 Wolfr. Look upwards, how 'tis thick and full, how
  sprinkled,
This heaven, with the planets. Now, consider;
Which will you have? The sun's already taken,
But you may find an oar in the half moon,
Or drive the comet's dragons; or, if you'd be
Rather a little snug and quiet god,
A one-horse star is standing ready for you.
Choose, and then drink.

 Isbr.   If you are sane or sober,
What do you mean?

 Wolfr.   It is a riddle, sir,
Siegfried, your friend, can solve.

 Siegfr.   Some sorry jest.

 Wolfr. You'll laugh but palely at its sting, I think.
Hold the dog down; disarm him; grasp his right.
My lord, this worthy courtier loved your virtues

To such excess of piety, that he wished
To send you by a bye-path into heaven.
Drink, and you're straight a god—or something else.
A conspirator. O murderous villain! Kill him
    where he sits.
  Isbr. Be quiet, and secure him. Siegfried, Siegfried;
Why hast thou no more genius in thy villany?
Wilt thou catch kings in cobwebs? Lead him hence:
Chain him to-night in prison, and to-morrow
Put a cord round his neck and hang him up,
In the society of the old dog
That killed my neighbour's sheep.
  Siegfr.   I do thank thee.
In faith, I hoped to have seen grass grow o'er you,
And should have much rejoiced. But, as it is,
I'll willingly die upright in the sun:
And I can better spare my life than you.
Good night then, Fool and Duke: you have my curse;
And Hell will have you some day down for hers:
So let us part like friends. My lords, good sleep
This night, the next I hope you'll be as well
As I shall. Should there be a lack of rope,
I recommend my bowstring as a strong one.
Once more, farewell: I wish you all, believe me,
Happily old, mad, sick, and dead, and cursed.
                  [Exit guarded.
  Isbr. That gentleman should have applied his talent
To writing new-year's wishes. Another cup!
            M

Wolfr. He has made us dull : so I'll begin a story.
As I was newly dead, and sat beside
My corpse, looking on it, as one who muses
Gazing upon a house he was burnt out of,
There came some merry children's ghosts, to play
At hide-and-seek in my old body's corners :—

Isbr. But how came you to die and yet be here ?

Wolfr. Did I say so ? Excuse me.   I am absent,
And forget always that I'm just now living.
But dead and living, which are which ?   A question
Not easy to be solved.   Are you alone,
Men, as you're called, monopolists of life ?
Or is all being, living ? and *what is*,
With less of toil and trouble, more alive,
Than they, who cannot, half a day, exist
Without repairing their flesh mechanism ?
Or do you owe your life, not to this body,
But to the sparks of spirit that fly off,
Each instant disengaged and hurrying
From little particles of flesh that die ?
If so, perhaps you are the dead yourselves :
And these ridiculous figures on the wall
Laugh, in their safe existence, at the prejudice,
That you are anything like living beings.
But hark !   The bell tolls, and a funeral comes.

(*A funeral procession crosses the stage ; the
pall borne by ladies.*)

Dirge.

We do lie beneath the grass
    In the moonlight, in the shade
Of the yew-tree. They that pass
    Hear us not. We are afraid
        They would envy our delight,
        In our graves by glow-worm night.
Come follow us, and smile as we;
    We sail to the rock in the ancient waves,
Where the snow falls by thousands into the sea,
    And the drowned and the shipwrecked have
        happy graves.

                    (*The procession passes out.*

Duke. What's this that comes and goes, so shadow-
    like?

Attendant. They bear the fair Sibylla to her grave.

Duke.   She dead!
Darest thou do this, thou grave-begotten man,
Thou son of Death?   (*To Wolfram.*

Wolfr.   Sibylla dead already?
I wondered how so fair a thing could live:
And, now she is no more, it seems to me
She was too beautiful ever to die!

Isbr. She, who was to have been my wife? Here,
    fellow;
Take thou this flower to strew upon her grave,
A lily of the valley; it bears bells,

For even the plants, it seems, must have their fool,
So universal is the spirit of folly;
And whisper, to the nettles of her grave,
" King Death hath asses' ears."

 Mario. (stabbing Isbrand) At length thou art
   condemned to punishment
Down, thou usurper, to the earth and grovel!
The pale form, that has led me up to thee,
Bids me deal this; and, now my task is o'er,
Beckons me hence.   [*Exit.*

 Isbr.   Villain, thou dig'st deep:
But think you I will die? Can I, that stand
So strong and powerful here, even if I would,
Fall into dust and wind? No: should I groan,
And close my eyes, be fearful of me still.
'Tis a good jest: I but pretend to die,
That you may speak about me bold and loudly;
Then I come back and punish: or I go
To dethrone Pluto. It is wine I spilt,
Not blood, that trickles down.

    Enter THORWALD *with soldiers.*

 Thorw. Long live duke Melveric, our rightful
   sovereign!
Down with the traitorous usurper, Isbrand!

 All. Long live duke Melveric!

 Isbr.   Duke Isbrand, long live he!
Duke Melveric is deposed.

Thorw.   Receive the homage
Of your revolted city.
    Duke.   Thorwald, thanks.
The usurper has his death-wound.
    Thorw.   Then cry, Victory!
And Long life to duke Melveric! once more.
    Isbr. I will live longer: when he's dead and buried,
A hundred years hence, or, it may be, more,
I shall return and take my dukedom back.
Imagine not I'm weak enough to perish:
The grave, and all its arts, I do defy.
    Wolfr. Meantime Death sends you back this cap of
office.
At his court you're elected to the post:
Go, and enjoy it.
        (He sets the fool's cap on Isbrand's head.
    Isbr. Bye and bye.   But let not
Duke Melveric think that I part unrevenged:
For I hear in the clouds about me voices,
Singing

> *All kingdomless is thy old head,*
>   *In which began the tyrannous fun;*
> *He fetches thee, who should be dead;*
>   *There's Duke for Brother! Who has won?*

I jest and sing, and yet alas! am he,
Who in a wicked masque would play the Devil;

But jealous Lucifer himself appeared,
And bore him—whither? I shall know to-morrow,
For now Death makes indeed a fool of me.   [*dies.*

  Duke. Where are my sons? I have not seen them
    lately.
Go to the bridegroom's lodgings, and to Athulf's,
And summon both.   [*Exit attendant.*

  Wolfr.   They will be here; and sooner
Than you would wish. Meanwhile, my noble Duke,
Some friends of mine behind us seem to stir.
They wish, in honour of your restoration,
In memory also of your glorious deeds,
To present masque and dance to you. Is't granted?

  Duke. Surely; and they are welcome, for we need
Some merriment amid these sad events.

  Wolfr. You in the wall there then, my thin light
    archers,
Come forth and dance a little: 'tis the season
When you may celebrate Death's Harvest-home.

    (*A dance of Deaths. In the middle of it enter*
    AMALA, *followed by a bier, on which the*
    corpse of Adalmar is borne. The dance goes
    out.)

  Duke. What's this? Another mummery?

  Wolfr.   The antimasque,
I think they call it; 'tis satirical.

  Amala. My lord, you see the bridal bed that waits me.
Your son, my bridegroom, both no more, lies here,

Cold, pale, abandoned in his youthful blood :
And I his bride have now no duty else,
But to kneel down, wretched, beside his corpse,
Crying for justice on his murderers.

   Duke. Could my son die, and I not know it sooner ?
Why, he is cold and stiff. O ! now my crown
Is sunk down to the dust, my life is desolate.
Who did this deed ?

Enter Athulf.

   Wolfr.   Athulf, answer thou !
   Amala. O no ! Suspect not him. He was last night
Gentle, and full of love, to both of us,
And could imagine ne'er so foul a deed.
Suspect not him ; for so thou mak'st me feel
How terrible it is that he is dead,
Since his next friend's accused of such a murder :
And torture not his ghost, which must be here,
Striving in vain to utter one soul-sound,
To speak the guiltless free.   Tempt not cruelly
The helplessness of him who is no more,
Nor make him discontented with the state,
Which lets him not assert his brother's innocence.

   Duke. (to Athulf.) Answer ! Thou look'st like
        one, unto whose soul
A secret voice, all day and night, doth whisper,
" Thou art a murderer." Is it so ? Then rather
Speak not.   Thou wear'st a dagger at thy side ;

Avenge the murdered man, thou art his brother;
And never let me hear from mortal lips
That my son was so guilty.

   Athulf.   Amala,
Still love me; weep some gentle drops for me;
And, when we meet again, fulfil thy promise.
Father, look here!

      (He kisses Amala's hand and stabs himself.

   Amala. O Athulf! live one moment to deny it;
I ask that, and that only. Lo! old man,
He hath in indignation done the deed.
Since thou could'st think him for an instant guilty,
He held the life, which such a base suspicion
Had touched, and the old father who could think it,
Unworthy of him more: and he did well.
I bade thee give me vengeance for my bridegroom,
And thou hast slain the only one who loved me.
Suspect and kill me too: but there's no need;
For such a one, as I, God never let
Live more than a few hours.

      (She falls into the arms of her ladies.

   Duke. Thorwald, the crown is yours; I reign no more.
But when, thou spectre, is thy vengeance o'er?

   Wolfr. Melveric, all is finished, which to witness
The spirit of retribution called me hither.
Thy sons have perished for like cause, as that
For which thou did'st assassinate thy friend.
Sibylla is before us gone to rest.

Blessing and Peace to all who are departed !
But thee, who daredst to call up into life,
And the unholy world's forbidden sunlight,
Out of his grave him who reposed softly,
One of the ghosts doth summon, in like manner,
Thee, still alive, into the world o' th' dead.

(Exit with the Duke into the sepulchre.

The curtain falls.

L'ENVOI.

WHO findeth comfort in the stars and flowers
    Apparelling the earth and evening sky,
That moralize throughout their silent hours,
And woo us heaven-wards till we wish to die;
Oft hath he singled from the soothing quire,
For its calm influence, one of softest charm
To still his bosom's pangs, when they desire
A solace for the world's remorseless harm.
Yet they, since to be beautiful and bless
Is but their way of life, will still remain
Cupbearers to the bee in humbleness,
Or look untouched down through the moony rain,
Living and being worlds in bright content,
Ignorant, not in scorn, of his affection's bent.

So thou, whom I have gazed on, seldom seen,
Perchance forgotten to the very name,
Hast in my thoughts the living glory been,
In beauty various, but in grace the same.
At eventide, if planets were above,
Crowning anew the sea of day bereft,
Swayed by the dewy heaviness of love,
My heart felt pleasure in the track thou'dst left:

And so all sights, all musings, pure and fair,
Touching me, raised thy memory to sight,
As· the sea-suns awakes the sun in air,—
If they were not reflections, thou the light.
Therefore bend hitherwards, and let thy mildness
Be glassed in fragments through this storm and wildness.

And pardon, if the sick light of despair
Usurp thy semblance oft, with tearful gleam
Displaying haunted shades of tangled care
In my sad scenes : soon shall a pearly beam,
Shed from the forehead of my heaven's queen,—
That front thy hand is pressed on,—bring delight.
Nor frown, nor blame me, if, such charms between,
Spring mockery, or thoughts of dreadest night.
Death's darts are sometimes Love's. So Nature tells,
When laughing waters close o'er drowning men ;
When in flowers' honied corners poison dwells ;
When Beauty dies : and the unwearied ken,
Of those who seek a cure for long despair,
Will learn. Death hath his dimples everywhere ;
Love only on the cheek, which is to me most fair.

NOTES.

THE historical fact, on which the preceding drama may be considered as founded, viz. that a Duke of Munsterberg in Silesia was stabbed to death by his court-fool, is to be found in Flögel's Gesch. d. Hoffnarren Liegnitz v. Leipzig 1789. 8. S. 297 u. folg.

Page 91, line 21.

' Aldabaron, called by the Hebrews Luz.'

As this antiquity in osteological history seems to have been banished from anatomical works since the good old days of Bartholinus and Kulmus, it will perhaps be agreeable to the curious reader to find here some notice of it, collected out of the rabbinical writings, &c. by the author's Russian friend Bernhard Reich, whose knowledge of the science and language renders him singularly capable of such investigations.

The bone Luz (לוז) is, according to the Rabbins, the only one which withstands dissolution after death, and out of which the body will be developed at the resurrection. A curious passage on the subject occurs in Berestieth raba.

Sect. 28, האדם כעת־ד לנא נמחדז אפילד לוז
שר שדרה שממע הקבה כעיק את

" Even the Luz of the shedrah, שדרה (*backbone*) out of " which God will hereafter raise the son of earth, is annihi- " lated." Old anatomists as Bartholinus, Vesalius, &c. mention it, but are not certain what bone was so designated, whether it is situated in the hand, foot, or vertebral column,

Luz לוּז is however beyond a doubt the os coccygis of the
osteologians, for the rabbins say that it lies under the 18th
Chulia חוליא vertebra. (Maaroch Hamarachot Article
לוּז), and it appears from various passages in the Talmud
that the vertebræ of the neck were not reckoned by the rabbinical writers to the vertebral column שדרה, but that
they began to count the latter from the first dorsal vertebra,
like Hippocrates (de ossium naturâ. V.) They say בשדרה
יח חוליות 18 vertebræ (chuliot) compose the shedrah
שדרה vertebral column—See Ohol. c. 1. Berach p. 30.
Now, if we reckon the twelve dorsal, five lumbal, vertebræ,
and the os sacrum together, we have the eighteen bones under
which Luz is to be found: Luz is therefore the os coccygis.
Etymology is also for this opinion; for Luz לוז is an almond; the Targum Jonathan translates in many places the
Hebrew Shaked שקד almond, plural Sckedim שקדים
Luz and Luzin לוזין לוז (Num. 17. 23, &c.) The form
of the bone is really similar to that of an almond. In the
lexicon we find the explanation of the word given from
κόκκυξ, cuckoo, but this bird appears to have very little to do
with the bone, and it is probable that the term is derived by
some corruption from κοκκός, a nut or the seed of any tree.

FINIS.

PRINTED BY C. WHITTINGHAM, CHISWICK.

PUBLICATIONS OF

WILLIAM PICKERING,

177, PICCADILLY.

(Opposite Burlington House.)

OMPLETE Works of George Her-
bert in Verse and Prose. With his Life by Izaak
Walton. In 2 vols. demy 8vo. handsomely printed
by Whittingham, 1*l.* 1*s.*

This Edition is printed with large type, and in-
tended for the Library. Copies may be had in
appropriate bindings.

The Same, 2 vols. fcp. 8vo. 5s. each Volume.

Taylor's Rule and Exercise of Holy Living and
Holy Dying, in 2 vols. *Octavo.* Printed by Whittingham, with
large type, price 1*l.* 1*s.* uniformly with the *Octavo* edition of
George Herbert's Works.

The Same, 2 vols. fcp. 8vo. 5s. each Volume.

Bishop Taylor's great Exemplar of Sanctity and
Holy Life, described in the History of the Life and Death of
the ever blessed Jesus Christ the Saviour of the World. 3
vols. fcp. 8vo. 13*s.* 6*d.*

The Pilgrim's Progress from this World to that
which is to come. By *John Bunyan.* Uniformly printed with
the *Octavo* Edition of George Herbert's Works. 8vo. price
10*s.* 6*d.*

The Sacred Poems and Private Ejaculations of
Henry Vaughan. With a Memoir by the Rev. H. F. Lyte,
fcp. 8vo. 5*s.*

" Preserving all the piety of George Herbert, they have less
of his quaint and fantastic turns, with a much larger infusion
of poetic feeling and expression."

The Life of Mrs. Godolphin, by John Evelyn, of
Wootton, Esq. Now first published. Edited by Samuel, Lord
Bishop of Oxford, Chancellor of the Most Noble Order of the
Garter. *Third Edition,* fcp. 8vo. with Portrait, 6*s.*

VII. Biographia Literaria, or Biographical
Sketches of my Literary Life and Opinions. Second Edition;
prepared for publication in part by the late H. N. Coleridge,
completed and published by his Widow, 3 vols. fcp. 8vo. 18s.

VIII. Notes and Lectures upon Shakespeare, and
some of the Old Poets and Dramatists, with other Literary Remains. Edited by Mrs. H. N. Coleridge. 2 vols. fcp. 8vo. 12s.

IX. Literary Remains, Edited by H. N. Cole-
ridge, 4 vols. 8vo. (Vols. I. and II. out of print.) Vols. 3 and 4,
12s. each.
 Contents.—Vol. III. Formula of the Trinity; Nightly
Prayer; Notes on the Book of Common Prayer, Hooker, Field,
Donne, Henry More, Heinrichs, Hacket, Jeremy Taylor, The
Pilgrim's Progress, John Smith, &c.—Vol. IV. Notes on Lu-
ther, St. Theresa, Bedell, Baxter, Leighton, Sherlock, Water-
land, Skelton, Andrew Fuller, Whitaker, Oxlee, A Barrister's
Hints, Davison, Irving, and Noble; and an Essay on Faith, &c.

Phantasmion, a Tale, by Sara Coleridge. Fcp.
8vo. 9s.
 " 'Phantasmion' is not a poem; but it is poetry from beginning to end, and has many poems within it. A Fairy Tale
unique in its kind, pure as a crystal in diction, tinted like the
opal with the hues of an everspringing sunlit fancy."—*Quar-
terly Review.*

Pickering's Aldine Edition of the Poets. Price
5s. each volume, in cloth boards, or 10s. 6d. bound in morocco
by Hayday. Each author may be had separately; or complete
sets, 53 volumes, price 13l. 5s. in boards.

Akenside.	H. Kirke White.
Beattie.	Milton, 3 vols.
Burns, 3 vols.	Parnell.
Butler, 2 vols.	Pope, 3 vols.
Chaucer, 6 vols.	Prior, 2 vols.
Churchill, 3 vols.	Shakespeare.
Collins.	Spenser, 5 vols.
Cowper, 3 vols.	Surrey and Wyatt, 2 vols.
Dryden, 5 vols.	Swift, 3 vols.
Falconer.	Thomson, 2 vols.
Goldsmith.	Young, 2 vols.
Gray.	

 " A complete collection of our Poets, with well written Me-
moirs, and good readable type is a desideratum; and from the
works sent forth we feel assured that the Aldine Edition will
supply the want."—*Athenæum.*

Trieste Publishing has a massive catalogue of classic book titles. Our aim is to provide readers with the highest quality reproductions of fiction and non-fiction literature that has stood the test of time. The many thousands of books in our collection have been sourced from libraries and private collections around the world.

The titles that Trieste Publishing has chosen to be part of the collection have been scanned to simulate the original. Our readers see the books the same way that their first readers did decades or a hundred or more years ago. Books from that period are often spoiled by imperfections that did not exist in the original. Imperfections could be in the form of blurred text, photographs, or missing pages. It is highly unlikely that this would occur with one of our books. Our extensive quality control ensures that the readers of Trieste Publishing's books will be delighted with their purchase. Our staff has thoroughly reviewed every page of all the books in the collection, repairing, or if necessary, rejecting titles that are not of the highest quality. This process ensures that the reader of one of Trieste Publishing's titles receives a volume that faithfully reproduces the original, and to the maximum degree possible, gives them the experience of owning the original work.

We pride ourselves on not only creating a pathway to an extensive reservoir of books of the finest quality, but also providing value to every one of our readers. Generally, Trieste books are purchased singly - on demand, however they may also be purchased in bulk. Readers interested in bulk purchases are invited to contact us directly to enquire about our tailored bulk rates. Email: customerservice@triestepublishing.com

You May Also Like

The Business of Being a Friend

Bertha Conde

ISBN: 9781760571597
Paperback: 144 pages
Dimensions: 6.14 x 0.31 x 9.21 inches
Language: eng

Handbook for Southport : Medical and General, with Copious Notices of the Natural History of the District

Edward Day McNicoll

ISBN: 9781760579760
Paperback: 194 pages
Dimensions: 6.14 x 0.41 x 9.21 inches
Language: eng

You May Also Like

THE MARITIME MEDICAL NEWS

Unknown

Trieste

The Maritime medical news

Unknown

ISBN: 9780649077274
Paperback: 70 pages
Dimensions: 6.14 x 0.14 x 9.21 inches
Language: eng

A LOST CHAPTER IN THE HISTORY OF MARY QUEEN OF SCOTS RECOVERED: NOTICES OF JAMES, EARL OF BOTHWELL, AND LADY JANE GORDONE, AND OF THE DISPENSATION FOR THEIR MARRIAGE; REMARKS ON THE LAW AND PRACTICE OF SCOOTLAND RELATIVE TO MARRIAGE DISPENSATIONS

John Stuart

Trieste

A Lost Chapter in the History of Mary Queen of Scots Recovered: Notices of James, Earl of Bothwell, and Lady Jane Gordone, and of the Dispensation for Their Marriage; Remarks on the Law and Practice of Scootland Relative to Marriage Dispensations

John Stuart

ISBN: 9781760575496
Paperback: 136 pages
Dimensions: 6.14 x 0.29 x 9.21 inches
Language: eng

www.triestepublishing.com

You May Also Like

Memoir of Keopuolani, Late Queen of the Sandwich Islands

William Richards

ISBN: 9781760570453
Paperback: 68 pages
Dimensions: 6.14 x 0.14 x 9.21 inches
Language: eng

Fugitive Poetry

N. P. Willis

ISBN: 9781760579159
Paperback: 104 pages
Dimensions: 6.14 x 0.22 x 9.21 inches
Language: eng

You May Also Like

Elektra

Sophocles

ISBN: 9780649019144
Paperback: 80 pages
Dimensions: 6.14 x 0.17 x 9.21 inches
Language: eng

Rab and His Friends

John Brown

ISBN: 9780649019175
Paperback: 78 pages
Dimensions: 6.14 x 0.16 x 9.21 inches
Language: eng

Find more of our titles on our website. We have a selection of thousands of titles that will interest you. Please visit

www.triestepublishing.com